Sydney froze, staring into the shiny chrome muzzle of the gun. A 9-millimeter Ruger, she surmised. During the past several months she'd learned all about guns. Their makes and models. How to load, shoot, and clean them. Even how to conceal them on her body. But there was one thing her studies hadn't covered: how it felt when one was pointed directly at you.

A lot of good those months of training had done her. She knew she should be able to find a way out of this. But then fear slid down her throat, forming a cold, hard ball in the pit of her stomach, preventing her from moving. Speaking. Breathing. And only one thought kept echoing in her panicked brain.

I'M NINETEEN. AND I'M GOING TO DIE. . . .

ALIAS™

RECRUITED

LYNN MASON

AN ORIGINAL PREQUEL NOVEL BASED ON THE
HIT SERIES CREATED BY J. J. ABRAMS

BANTAM BOOKS
NEW YORK ✶ TORONTO ✶ LONDON ✶ SYDNEY ✶ AUCKLAND

Alias: Recruited

A Bantam Book / October 2002
Text and cover art copyright © 2002 by Touchstone Television

ISBN: 0-553-49398-1

Visit us on the Web! www.randomhouse.com

Published simultaneously in the United States and Canada

Bantam Books is an imprint of Random House Children's Books, a
division of Random House, Inc. BANTAM BOOKS and the rooster
colophon are registered trademarks of Random House, Inc. Bantam
Books, 1540 Broadway, New York, New York 10036.

PRINTED IN THE UNITED STATES OF AMERICA

OPM 10 9 8 7 6 5 4 3 2

One of my biggest pet peeves is when people assume they know all about someone they've barely met. Take me, for example. I'm tall and thin and get my sensibly styled hair trimmed once a month (just a quarter inch, or if I'm feeling **risky**, a half inch, but only if Debbie is working that day—I can trust her).

Sometimes I wear tortoiseshell glasses that my best friend swears make me look like a librarian. On most days I can be seen carrying a backpack that weighs about thirty pounds. I don't drink or smoke. I'm athletic but prefer individual **competition** over team sports. I'd rather read *Jane Eyre* for the ninth time than the new issue of *Cosmopolitan*. I speak five languages (six if you count pig latin).

From these few details, people assume that I'm a brainiac. That I have no life. That I live in a world of books. That I spout off foreign phrases in my sleep. That I take too many solitary jogs.

You know what's pathetic? They're right.

But it's the start of my freshman year. Something out there is **waiting** for me. Some sort of higher calling or purpose or . . . or something. I can feel it. And I'm about to find out who—or what—it is. . . .

"YOU ARE *NOT NORMAL!*" Francie screeched, waving a pale-pink-tipped finger at Sydney. "What kind of person takes Spanish *and* Chinese as electives?"

Sydney Bristow rolled her eyes, but a soft smile stole across her mouth. She'd only known Francie Calfo since the summer and already she was used to these occasional flare-ups. With her melodic voice and her flair for the dramatic, Francie could easily turn an everyday conversation into a highly charged debate.

"Tell her, Baxter," Francie said, elbowing her

new boyfriend's lean, basketball-player arms. "Tell her that you're supposed to take electives like Famous French Films or Ballroom Dancing when you're a freshman."

"Hey, man, I'm staying out of it," Baxter replied, lifting his large hands in a gesture of surrender. "You two just keep on talking. I'm going to keep an eye out for that guy who sells ice cream." He swiveled around on the bench and leaned against the table, checking out the UCLA scene on a sunny September day.

"Come on, Fran. I like languages," Sydney said, turning her eyes back to her Spanish textbook. "I'm good at them. And besides, if I hope to get a teaching fellowship in a foreign country someday, it'll improve my odds."

Francie leaned forward. "Yes, but will it help you get guys?"

Sydney laughed. "I don't know. Foreign guys, maybe." She wished Francie would give it a rest. Ever since she'd started dating Baxter a couple of weeks ago, Francie had seemed intent on finding Sydney a guy of her own. Sydney had to admit she wouldn't mind either. But with one exception, she hadn't met any guys she would even consider going out with.

"So you're serious about this master teacher

plan, huh?" Francie asked through a mouthful of salad. "You really see yourself standing in front of a classroom molding hundreds of minds? Young, obnoxious, sex-crazed minds?"

"Speak for yourself," Sydney said, stretching back so that her white T-shirt rose slightly over her non-pierced navel. Although she wouldn't say so to Francie, she'd actually been trying to picture herself in that very position. Giving lectures at a podium. Scrawling passages from Sartre across dusty blackboards. Gossiping with the other overworked, underpaid teachers in cramped, coffee-cup-strewn lounges. Doing the whole teacher thing.

Only one thing was wrong with her mental picture. It wasn't happening for her. Not good for an education major.

Sydney had been looking forward to college forever. She had sailed through her college boards, so she hadn't had to suffer through any of UCLA's required courses. So far she was having no trouble with her classes. It was the students who were daunting. Everyone here was a standout—high school valedictorians (she among them), goal-scoring quarterbacks, computer geeks, drama queens, and rah-rah cheerleaders, all trying to fit in.

Not that she'd gotten to know anybody. Nope,

out of the, oh, 30,000 students or so at UCLA, Sydney knew a whopping total of three: Francie, Baxter, and her friend from track, Todd de Rossi. The introductory courses, with their large lecture halls and even larger lecture groups, overwhelmed her. And while she had never been intimidated by brilliance, being around faculty members who were among the top scholars and scientists in the United States was a bit unsettling. She had witnessed upperclassmen engaging in lively debates and discussions with professors in the halls or as they walked across Dickson Plaza. One day, she'd overheard a professor offer to meet with a student over coffee to discuss a problem he was having. The professor's generosity impressed her—and made her wistful.

I bet Mom was like that, Sydney thought now, clicking her pen open and shut. Laura Bristow had been a highly regarded professor of literature at UCLA. She had had a passion for learning and for teaching. But that was before she died in a car accident when Sydney was six.

It had been a typical, hazy Friday night in Los Angeles. Sydney's parents had gone out to the movies while she stayed home with her nanny. A car had come from the opposite direction, crossing over the road's centerline. Her father had swerved to avoid it, and had careened off a bridge. He had survived. Her mother had not.

"She didn't have time to know what was happening," Sydney's father had told her tiny, heartbroken six-year-old self, as if that small consolation made it all better.

Dad. Calm, cool, and utterly disconnected. The man was capable of smiling—there was proof of that in a sterling-silver-Tiffany-framed photograph he kept on top of his bedroom dresser of him and her mom and Sydney one sunny day in Venice. Mom, her hands on Sydney's bare, slightly peeling shoulders, laughing with her mouth half open. Sydney, holding a dripping ice cream cone, a smudge of chocolate on her chin, wearing that tank top with the rainbow decal. Dad, smiling over at his wife, at her obvious happiness.

Sydney couldn't remember ever seeing that smile in the flesh.

After her mother died, Sydney had grown up under her father's distant eye, spending more time isolated with her books than with family or friends. As time passed, her recollections of her mother faded. Just a few memories remained. . . . Catching fireflies in old applesauce jars with holes punched in the lids on a hot summer night. Riding the Matterhorn at Disneyland, screaming and laughing at the same time. Baking brownies and taking turns licking the orange Pyrex bowl clean. Watching her mother, her long dark glossy hair pulled back in a chignon, thumb through her collection of large, beautifully leather-bound books—a gift from her father that was now part of Sydney's own library.

It hadn't taken long for Francie to speculate that Sydney wanted to become a teacher not because she had a deep-seated passion to teach, but as a way to honor her mother's memory.

Was Francie right? Probably.

When she had been paired up with Francie at a special freshman orientation held at the beginning of summer, Sydney had been shy. She'd never been one to have lots of friends, and the bubbly, outgoing Francie had intimidated her. But there was something about Francie that made Sydney open up, and soon she had found herself spilling all sorts of things to her. Francie had confided in her as well, and by the time fall term began the two were fast friends—and roommates.

"Come on, Syd. I mean it," Francie said with a pout, startling Sydney from her thoughts. "You should seriously think about closing that textbook and decide what you're going to wear to the Tropical Getaway party Friday night. We've been looking forward to it for weeks."

Sydney sighed. *"Bien. ¿Por que no?"* She closed her book and slid it into her backpack.

"Good girl," Francie said approvingly. "Now, are you going in your hula skirt or that flowered sarong?"

"I don't know. The sarong, I guess."

"Excellent. So can I borrow your hula skirt to wear over my bikini? Please?" Francie asked, raising a hopeful eyebrow.

"Hey, I like the sound of that," Baxter observed, turning back around.

"Oh!" Francie exclaimed, pointing at Baxter. "And then we can all three wear matching leis! Won't that be cool?"

"Uh . . . I don't know about that," Baxter said, his grin disappearing. "I don't think I want to be all matching and wearing flowers around my teammates. The dudes'll call me Martha Stewart for the rest of the year."

Francie rolled her eyes. "Sydney. Will you please tell him that we've progressed as a society and that men don't judge other men by what they wear anymore?"

"Actually, you haven't met my friend Todd," Sydney said. "He's always finding fashion emergencies."

"Thank you, Sydney," Baxter confirmed. "Now, if you two lovely ladies will excuse me, I've got to start trekking across campus for my history class. Catch you later." He leaned in and gave Francie a long kiss. Sydney looked down at her soggy salad and began rearranging lettuce leaves with her fork.

After what seemed like a mini-eternity, Baxter grabbed his backpack and began loping down the sidewalk. "Bye," Francie called in a breathy voice. Then she turned back toward Sydney and flashed her a huge grin. "Isn't he amazing? I am really looking forward to the party. The three of us are going to have a blast!"

"Yeah," said Sydney, drawing the word out slowly. Being a third wheel on Francie's date. What a hoot. "You know, I've gotta ask. Are you sure you want me tagging along?"

"Syd." Francie blew out her breath. "You won't be tagging along. We *want* you to come. Of course . . ." She smiled slyly. "You could always ask someone to come with you and make it a four-some. Maybe that certain someone in your litera-ture class?"

Not this again, Sydney thought, taking a long

sip of her bottled water. Definitely time to change the subject. "Oh, hey, can I see your newspaper?" she asked, nodding toward the folded copy of the *Los Angeles Register* lying in front of Francie.

"Sure," Francie replied, handing it over. "Why?"

"I need a job." Sydney quickly found the employment section and spread it open.

"A job?" Francie repeated. "But I thought you had a scholarship?"

"I do," Sydney said, her eyes slowly roving down the columns of ads. "Only it doesn't cover all my expenses. And I *don't* want to be calling up my dad all the time asking for money."

"Right," Francie said in a hushed voice.

Sydney was glad she didn't have to explain. Francie already knew well enough how difficult Jack Bristow could be. During their late-night talks, Sydney had opened up to her friend about her cold relationship with her father.

Johnathan "Jack" Bristow was a difficult man, to say the least. Always so caught up in his job at Jennings Aerospace as an airplane parts exporter, he never had much time for Sydney. On parent days the only person who would show up to see her was her former nanny. Letters from home consisted of signed checks with no notes attached.

Now that she was a declared psych major, Francie was always spouting off new psychobabble. To her, it was plain that Sydney's father had never recovered from his wife's accidental death. And the fact that Sydney resembled her mother so much only reminded him of the pain.

Maybe. It wasn't like Sydney had ever discussed it with him. Or ever would.

Sydney often took out the few precious photos she had of her mom and studied them closely. She and her mother had the same full, curvy lips, deep-set dark eyes, long, angular jawline, and abundance of chestnut brown hair. The main difference was the expression. In both the photos and Sydney's dim memories, her mother was always laughing and smiling. Sydney was more reserved—besides her height, it was the only trait she could trace directly to her father.

"See anything good?" Francie asked, pointing her cracker toward the paper.

Sydney shook her head. "Telemarketing . . . telemarketing . . . one that requires heavy lifting . . . fry cook . . . hairdresser . . . *ugh!* Here's one that says, 'Professional photographer seeks hairy females.'"

"Yuck!" Francie exclaimed. "Wonder what his deal is."

"Looks like I'm out of luck," Sydney muttered, resting her chin on her fists. "I can't cook or give perms and I'm not particularly hairy. And the thought of selling stuff over the phone makes me want to retch."

"I've got it!" Francie whacked her forehead with the palm of her hand. "Why didn't I think of it before? We need another waitress down at the restaurant. You should come and apply tomorrow when I go to work!"

"Are you sure?" Sydney asked, wrinkling her nose. "I've never waitressed before. I've never done much of anything, actually."

"Not a problem. Aren't you great at every-thing?"

"Learning to say 'Have a nice day' in Mandarin is one thing," Sydney said. "Dealing with a surly short-order cook named Bubba is another."

Francie gave her a look. "Let me say the magic word: *tips*." She grinned. "That's the thing about waitressing. Some days it feels like the worst job in the world, but there's no other gig where you can leave with a wad of cash in your pocket."

Sydney waggled her eyebrows.

"Oh, stop," Francie admonished, laughing. "A *legit* job. It would be cool working together, don't you think?" she pressed.

Sydney nodded, slowly at first, then faster. "Okay, I'll do it." She dove her fork back into her salad and began scooping out the soggy croutons— her favorite part. Okay. Waiting tables wasn't exactly her dream job, but it would at least give her some financial independence. And maybe, just maybe, it could give her a life beyond books.

All of a sudden, Francie reached out and grabbed Sydney's forearm. "Don't look now," she whispered, "but here he comes."

Sydney didn't need to look to know who Francie was referring to. His image had been seared into her brain ever since the first day of school, when he had sat down beside her and asked to borrow a pen—which he never returned. It was sad, she knew, but she actually got a secret thrill each time she saw him hold what she believed was her black Sharpie in his slightly calloused fingers.

She couldn't resist the chance to . . . experience him now. To catch sight of thick blond waves framing unusually large green eyes. Tanned skin that seemed to give off its own heat. Dimpled cheeks, and a cleft down the middle of his chin, like a scalloped edge on a piece of fine art.

Guys like Dean Carothers didn't grow on orange trees. He was special, one of those rare human beings who belonged in an Abercrombie & Fitch ad. In a body-baring music video with pulsating beats accentuating his every move. Sipping café au lait in Paris, a scarf wrapped around his neck, his glossy hair mussed by the breeze.

Primal attraction aside, there was something else about Dean that drew Sydney to him like a honeybee to nectar. It was the way he moved, with the assurance of someone who was very used to getting his own way, radiating self-confidence with his constant smile and fluid, effortless movements. The type of guy who saw what he wanted and went for it. She couldn't help admiring that. Among other things.

He was now just a few feet away. A sizzling sensation crept over her neck and cheeks. Instinctively, she propped up her Spanish textbook and ducked behind it.

"Syd!" Francie scolded in a loud whisper. "Don't hide from the guy. Go over there and say hi."

"Why? I'll just end up acting stupid," Sydney mumbled, peering furtively around her book as Dean sauntered past, all broad shoulders and high-wattage smiles for lucky passersby. She had never had a real boyfriend. Being around guys that were even one-tenth as beautiful as Dean had always made her feel brainy and tongue-tied and a variety of other emotions that were definitely not good ones.

"You will not," Francie countered. "Come on. Go over and ask him to the party."

Sydney shook her head. "It's not that easy. I can't just ask him out of the blue like that."

"Why not? You said he talks to you all the time in class, right?"

"Well, yeah. But he's just asking about my notes or the essay assignment," Sydney replied, wishing that she were just being modest. "Nothing major."

"So?" Francie cried. "He's probably been flirting with you all this time and you don't even realize it."

Sydney chuckled. Since when had Francie started taking drugs? Guys like Dean didn't flirt with her. They didn't do anything with her. "I don't think so, Fran."

"Listen to me." Francie leaned forward and stared directly into her eyes. "Just go over there and talk to the guy. That's all. This party is the perfect excuse to try and hook up. And right now when he's alone is the perfect time to approach him."

Sydney bowed her head and risked a casual

glance over her shoulder. Dean was sitting at a shady picnic table all by himself, without the group of people who typically trailed in his wake. Francie was right. If she ever wanted to talk to him privately, this was her chance.

She shot Francie a helpless look. "You really think I should?"

Francie grinned. "Go for it now, before you change your brilliant mind."

"Okay." Taking a deep breath, Sydney pushed herself up and forced her legs to carry her toward him.

As she neared his table, Dean glanced up at her.

"Hi," she said, twisting a lock of hair around a finger, holding it like a lifeline.

"Hey," he said, smiling slightly. "What's up?"

Sydney felt her own mouth curl upward in response, warmth returning to her cheeks. His smile was just the sign she needed to top off her courage. She shrugged her left shoulder. "Not much. Have you, uh . . ." She paused, gathering her nerve. "Have you heard about the Tropical Getaway party?"

"Yeah, sure," he replied, casually swishing the ice in his soda cup.

She nodded. "Cool. Um . . . so is it something you'd like to go to?"

"Yeah, I guess," he said with a shrug.

Sydney's heart sped to a full gallop. "You would?" Visions of Dean in Hawaiian swim trunks, a lei reaching down to his bare, suntanned abs and his arm drooped lazily around her shoulders, took over her brain.

"I don't know. Maybe. If I don't have anything else going on," he continued. He gazed up at her with eyes the color of emeralds. "Why? Are you doing a poll for the newspaper or something?"

A cold, tingly feeling spread through her. *Oh, god!* she thought. *He never even considered going out with me. I'm practically peeing my Levis over a guy who only thinks of me as Sharpie girl.*

"No," she attempted in a mumble. "No, I just . . ." But her throat was squeezing shut and she couldn't finish. All she wanted to do was run and hide. California was the land of earthquakes, but where were they when you needed one?

Comprehension gradually seeped into his super-human features. "Oh," he said, raising up from his slouched position. A bemused look crossed his face. "Are you asking me out, uh—sorry, what was your name again?"

"It's— No, really. I wasn't. I mean, no. I've gotta go," she blurted out, staring down at the chipped polish on her toenails. Barely There Red, wasn't it? Then she ripped her eyes away from all his Dean glory, turned, and walked back to Francie as fast as she could.

Kill me now, she thought. *Embarrassed* was too weak a word to describe what she was feeling. Her face must have told Francie everything, because she didn't ask what had happened. As Sydney sank down onto the bench, her friend threw a supportive arm around her shoulders and patted her. "Forget about it," she murmured. "He's not worth it."

Sydney could only sit there, mentally replaying the entire incident in horrific superslow motion. What was wrong with her? What had made her think she even had a chance with Dean? *Are you asking me out, uh—sorry, what was your name again? What's your name? Again? Again?* So he had talked to her a few times in class. So what? He wasn't interested. He was just nice.

Suddenly a high-pitched squeal cut through the noise in her mind. She turned around, following the sound, and saw a trio of girls who appeared to have just stepped out of a Tommy Hilfiger ad and a couple of scruffily cute guys she recognized from her economics class standing in a semicircle around Dean. All of them were looking right at her.

Laughing.

Obviously he *wasn't* nice.

"Come on," Francie said firmly. "We're leaving." Sydney's hands were shaking as she and Francie gathered up their things, hoisted their backpacks onto their shoulders, and made their way through the gap between the Geology and Math Sciences buildings.

"Don't worry, Syd," Francie said soothingly, laying a reassuring hand on her back. "You'll find someone who really deserves you. It'll go better next time."

Sydney didn't respond. Francie meant well, but she was wrong.

There wouldn't *be* a next time. Sydney would never take a chance like that again.

2

"I'M NOT SAYING IT'S like the best place to work, but it doesn't bite too hard. I mean, sometimes the customers can be rude, or gross, or ask for stupid things like a turkey sandwich without the bread. But really it's not too bad." Francie prattled on and on as they drove through the packed downtown parking lot Wednesday afternoon, searching for an empty space.

"Relax, Fran," Sydney said, pulling into a spot near the back. "Why are you so nervous?"

Francie shrugged, her left shoulder grazing a strand of long wavy black hair. "I don't know. I guess because it's my idea. I'd feel responsible if you absolutely hated it."

Sydney cut the engine. "Hey. You aren't forcing me here. You're helping me out. And I really, really appreciate it."

"Okay," Francie said, furrowing her brow at Sydney. "But if you totally despise the place, promise me you won't take the job just so I won't feel bad or anything."

"I promise," Sydney replied. With her lack of restaurant experience, she wasn't feeling too confident. But everyone had to start somewhere. "Hey, it's not like I have lots of job options anyway."

As they hopped out onto the pavement, Sydney locked the doors of her brand-new white Ford Mustang. Her dad had bought it for her before she went off to college. She definitely needed her own car if she was to have any life at UCLA, and without her dad's help she'd almost certainly have been driving a lemon from a place like Swappin' Steve's Gently Used Wheels. Still, it made her uncomfortable to accept such a generous gift from him. Every time she looked at it, she thought of him, and thinking of him was not something she allowed herself to do on a regular basis. The car was a huge reminder of the control he still had over her life—

at least financially. All the more reason for her to find a job.

They crossed the street and headed toward a squat, square building with a green-and-white-striped awning. A carved wooden sign overhead read LES AMIS CAFÉ in loopy red script.

As they walked through the front door, Sydney took a deep breath and closed her eyes. "*Mmmm. Thank god I don't have to live on dorm food alone. I swear, if you didn't bring back meals from this place now and then, I'd be seriously starved. Just smell that.*"

"I know. The best blintzes and strawberry cheesecake in town," Francie said with a smile.

"Hey! You never brought me cheesecake."

"Oh." Francie's face fell. "Well, I have. It's just never made it home."

"Francine!" a man called from the back of the café, where the kitchen and offices were located. As he approached, Sydney couldn't help thinking he looked like a human ferret, with his skinny build, thin face, long narrow nose, and beady brown eyes. He walked up to Francie, tapped his watch, and said, "Three and a half minutes late, Francine." Then he laughed awkwardly. "But who's counting?"

"Sorry, Mr. Terwilliger. Traffic was really bad today," Francie explained, mirroring his phony smile. "This is my friend Sydney. The one I told you about over the phone?"

Sydney took a step forward and held out her hand. "Hi. I'm Sydney Bristow."

Mr. Terwilliger grabbed her palm and began pumping it up and down. "Yes, yes, hello. Sydney, is it? It's very nice to meet you. Yes."

She hoped her revulsion wasn't too noticeable as Mr. Terwilliger maintained his limp, greasy grip. She felt a slight pang for Francie. For weeks she'd been complaining that her boss was a major weirdo, but Sydney had never pictured anything this bad. Eventually, he let go and gestured to a nearby door.

"Well then. Why don't we go into my office?" he said. "I have some forms for you to fill out."

"I'm going to go start my shift," Francie said, peering over her shoulder to give Sydney a reassuring smile. "Come find me when you're done."

Sydney entered the sparsely furnished wood-paneled office, discreetly wiping her palm on her linen skirt. She sat down in a squeaky red vinyl chair as Mr. Terwilliger plopped into his seat behind the desk.

"Here you go," he said, passing her a pen and a double-sided application form. As she bent over the sheet and began filling it out, she expected Mr. Terwilliger to excuse himself and say he'd come back later when she was done. Instead, he just sat there, swiveling back and forth in his chair and tapping his pen against the edge of his desk.

Sydney tried to ignore him, focusing as hard as she could on the questions in front of her. It didn't take long to fill in the blanks. The only real job she'd ever had was one horrible night spent babysitting her neighbor's three children.

"Let's see," Terwilliger muttered as she passed the form back to him. "Excellent grades. Yes. National Merit Finalist. Very nice. Scholarship . . ." He grew silent, his face slowly sagging as he scanned the rest of the document. Eventually he set down the application and tapped his fingertips together. "I take it you've never had a food service position before?" He said "food service" in a reverent tone, as if it were second on the world importance scale to finding a cure for cancer.

"Um, no," Sydney replied, her mind whirling. "But I did sell boxes of candy for a school fundraiser," she added with a hopeful smile. No need to tell him she'd only sold two chocolate bars—both to herself. "I also did some theater arts back at my high school, so I'm not shy around people. And I'm on the Bruins track team, which shows I'm coordinated. Right?" She continued to fix him with an enthusiastic grin, bracing for the eventual thanks-but-no-thanks dismissal.

"I see. Yes." Mr. Terwilliger intertwined his fingers and nodded slowly. After a few more minutes of reviewing her application, he smiled. "Well, Sydney," he said. "I think we could definitely use you on our staff."

Sydney gaped at his small, rodent eyes. "You mean I've got the job?"

"In fact, could you start today? We're a little shorthanded."

"Today?" she repeated, blinking rapidly. Had he actually offered her a job? Did Francie bribe him or something?

Mr. Terwilliger stood up and crossed the room. "There should be several spare uniforms in the storage closet. Don't worry, they're clean. I'll want you to train with Francie at first, then maybe you can go it alone after a couple of hours."

"That sounds great," Sydney said, a flush spreading across her cheeks. It was only a waitress position, she knew that, but the fact that someone found her worthy of employment, that someone (even if it was a human ferret) was willing to take a chance on her, filled her with an unexpected sense of pride. Thank god for Francie. Sydney walked over and reached out to shake her new boss's clammy hand. "Thanks. Thanks very much."

Mr. Terwilliger opened the office door and gestured outside. "You may not have a lot of experience, but I have a feeling about you, Sydney. I think we'll find you were born to do this job."

*   *   *

Five hours later Sydney was hiding behind the restaurant's gigantic stainless steel coffeemaker.

"How do you do it, Fran?" she asked in a whisper, while rubbing the heel of her left foot. The truth was, even though Francie had been nothing but encouraging, and Terwilliger had felt confident enough to hire her on the spot, Sydney was beginning to think she wasn't cut out for this job at all.

"Well, for one, I don't wear two-inch heels," Francie replied, checking her reflection in the burnished metal of the coffee machine. She smoothed her ponytail and straightened the collar of her Pepto-Bismol-pink uniform. "You're going to have to get some more comfortable shoes if you're going to do this."

"Hey, I was dressing for an interview. I had no idea I'd start today," Sydney retorted, moving on to her other foot. "Besides, that's not what I meant. What I wanted to know was, don't you ever feel . . ." She floundered for the right word.

"Majorly stressed?" Francie finished for her. "All the time. Don't worry, Syd. You're doing great. It takes a while to find your legs, then it's like you're on autopilot." She gave Sydney a reassuring pat on the shoulder and went back to measuring out the Colombian coffee grounds.

It's just a job, Sydney told herself as she slipped her shoes back on. *It's a way to break from Dad and stand on your own feet financially. If your feet can survive the first day.*

"You got that coffee brewed yet?" hollered a man from a nearby table.

"Just three more minutes, sir," Francie called back, smiling politely. Then she leaned toward Sydney and murmured, "Sounds to me like he should switch to decaf, don't you think?"

"Definitely," Sydney said, looking at Francie in amazement.

Francie made the job look almost fun. In fact,

Sydney had a brand-new respect for her friend. Francie joked with the customers and listened to their stories with real interest. She even knew some of the regulars by name. For the first two hours, Sydney had followed her around, learning things like how to tell the regular-brew coffee from the decaf (red versus blue carafe), how to write down orders in the shorthand the cooks were used to, and how to fold the flatware into the green cloth napkins. She'd even acquired the singsong cadence Francie used when greeting her customers. "*Hello, my name is Sydney and I'll be your waitress. Can I interest you in one of our award-winning* appetizers?" But somehow, she couldn't quite pick up Francie's positive attitude.

"So how's our rookie doing?" Sydney looked over and saw Robyn, one of their coworkers, a skinny redhead with a thick Texas drawl. She was standing on the other side of Francie, pushing an order slip through the window to the kitchen area. "You about ready to collapse yet?"

"She's doing great, aren't you, Syd?" Francie asked, nudging Sydney with her elbow. "For the past hour she's been handling those front booths all by herself. She's a natural."

"Really?" Robyn asked, loading several tumblers

of ice water onto her tray. "Everyone been treating you nice?"

Sydney nodded. "Pretty much."

"Well, if things get real boring, just do what I do." She hoisted her tray high over her head and started backing toward the dining room. "Just make a game of trying to figure out what people will order before they tell you. It's not exactly *Wheel of Fortune*, but it helps." She pivoted and walked off.

"Thanks. I'll try it," Sydney called after her. Then she picked up her own serving tray and smiled at Francie. "Okay. Here I go again."

"Only three more hours," Francie said encouragingly.

Sydney headed back to her assigned area, ready for a fresh start. She managed to ignore the throbbing in her feet as she refilled a coffee cup for a man at the bar, found a clean high chair for a young couple's wiggly toddler, and took back someone's supposedly overcooked fish.

Just as she was about to retreat behind the coffee-maker for another break, the front door swung open and Sydney could see a man silhouetted against the setting sun. He walked in and immediately sat down at one of the front booths she was assigned to cover. She took a good look at him, deciding to try Robyn's game and figure out what he might order. The man had thinning, stringy blond hair, a stocky build, and an extremely wide, pockmarked face. *Definitely one of our meat-and-potatoes platters,* she guessed. *With a cold beer to wash it down.*

As Sydney approached, the man straightened up and blatantly stared at her, his bleary blue eyes traveling down her body as she set a glass of ice water and a menu on the table.

"Hello," she greeted him, trying to sound as polite as possible. "*My* name is *Sydney,* and *I'll* be your waitress. Could I interest you—"

"Oh, you could interest me, all right, doll."

"—in some appetizers?" she finished through clenched teeth. "Perhaps some hot—"

"Yeah, I like things hot, all right."

"—shrimp quesadillas?"

"I'll tell you what, Cindy." He shut the menu and leaned forward, lowering his voice to a wheezy murmur. "Why don't you bring me a cup of coffee and then we'll talk about what I want."

Sydney's facial muscles ached from forcing herself to smile. "Right away, sir," she said, then quickly spun around and marched back to the wait station.

She veered around the wooden pillar separating

the wait station from the rest of the dining room. Francie and Robyn were there picking up orders.

"Excuse me, guys. Um, Francie? On a scale of one to ten, how angry would Mr. Terwilliger get if I dumped a pitcher of ice water in some guy's lap?"

"What? What guy?" Francie asked, glancing around.

"The creep in the corner."

Francie and Robyn craned their necks around the pillar and gasped simultaneously.

"Oh, no. That guy is the worst," Francie said, shaking her head. "Honey, I am so sorry. If I'd seen him come in, I would have dealt with him myself."

"You poor thing. I can't believe you're stuck with that asshole on your first day," Robyn muttered.

"So . . . you guys know him?"

"Unfortunately yes," Francie replied, rolling her eyes. "He comes in a lot. He always camps out at a table for like half a day and gives the waitress a hard time. It's like his reason to keep on living."

"Have you told Terwilliger?"

Robyn snorted. "He won't do anything. For one thing, he'd be too scared to approach the guy.

Besides, he always runs up a big bill. That's all Terwilliger cares about."

"Why don't I take over?" Francie said, taking a step toward the man. "I'm used to handling the jerk."

"No!" Sydney grasped her arm and pulled her back. "That wouldn't be fair. I've just got a row of booths and a couple of people at the bar to take care of. You guys each have half of the dining room."

At that moment a voice called out, "Hey! Cindy! I wanted that coffee now, doll. Not next summer."

Francie and Robyn gave her matching sympathetic looks.

"Don't worry," Sydney said, filling a large brown glazed mug with coffee. "I can handle him."

She cemented what she hoped was a friendly-yet-not-*too*-friendly smile on her face and strode back to the man's table. "Here you go," she said, setting the cup down in front of him. "So what can I get you?" she asked, reaching into her apron pocket for the order booklet.

The man's eyes twinkled maniacally. "How about your phone number?"

She tightened her grip on the pad and pencil and

took a deep breath. "Might I suggest a bowl of one of our homemade soups?" she asked. *Stay calm. Remember, you're getting paid way below minimum wage to put up with this crap.* "We have potato leek, chicken tortilla, gazpacho—"

"Just bring me one order of your legs," he interrupted with a devilish grin. "The honey-barbecue chicken legs. And be quick, doll. I'm a big tipper."

Just grin and bear it, she told herself as she retreated to the kitchen window to put in the order. *Just ignore his disgusting insinuations and do your job.*

When the food was ready, Sydney loaded up her tray, took a deep breath, and headed back. The man was still sitting there with the same leering expression he'd had when she left. Sydney averted her eyes and leaned across the table, setting out the warm plate and sauce bowl. All of a sudden she felt something brush against her right knee. She froze in horror and looked around. The creep was lazily holding his coffee in one hand and pawing the skirt of her uniform with the other.

Ugh! That's it! Without thinking, she slapped his hand away, whirled around, and rammed the thick plastic serving tray against him, pushing him upright. Lukewarm coffee splattered everywhere, most of it landing on him. She kept a tight grip on the tray, the rim of it hitting him right below his Adam's apple.

"Jeezus!" he cried hoarsely. His large meatball of a face had gone pale underneath the drops of coffee. And his bloodshot eyes were darting back and forth. Suddenly he didn't seem so menacing anymore—just utterly pathetic.

"Now let me give *you* a tip," she growled. "Find somewhere else to eat from now on. Or if you do come back, limit yourself to what's on the menu!"

"Yeah!" cried a woman a couple of tables over. A few others broke into applause, including Francie, who had crept closer for a better look. Robyn was standing near the kitchen, laughing into her hands.

"What's going on here?" shouted Mr. Terwilliger, barging out of the back office.

Whoops. Sydney quickly pulled back and set the tray on a nearby table. The man instantly jumped up from the booth, rubbing the thick red mark on his throat. "This waitress threatened me," he wheezed, waving a finger at Sydney. "I mean it! She's crazy!"

"Is this true?" Mr. Terwilliger said, glaring at Sydney.

"Mr. Terwilliger, he was abusive," Sydney began. "He actually—"

"Did you threaten one of our customers?" he repeated more loudly. The man was watching, his enraged eyes darting from Sydney to the human ferret.

Her stomach twisted. "Well, yes, but—"

"I'm afraid we cannot allow such behavior from a member of our waitstaff," he said with a pointed nod to the creep, his weasel-like features pinched into a stern frown. "I'd like you to leave."

"You mean . . . I'm fired?" Sydney asked, her voice quavering. She had always excelled at everything she did. . . . Was she really getting fired from a *waitress* position? Now that her anger had been unleashed, she felt shaky and worn out, and the realization of what she'd done was slowly sinking in. *What's wrong with you?* she cried inwardly. *Your friend gets you a job and you blow it in the first few hours?* That had to be some sort of record.

"Mr. Terwilliger, don't do this," Francie said, stepping forward. She lowered her voice. "This guy has had it coming for a long time."

A couple of onlookers shouted their agreement. Robyn looked down at the floor.

"This is not your decision to make, Francine," Mr. Terwilliger said, rounding on her. "I am the manager here. Get back to work."

"Damn straight," the asshole said self-righteously, sitting back down hard in his booth. "And somebody better get me my coffee. Pronto."

Sydney watched Francie's gaze harden and her hands close into fists. She knew those signs well. Any second now Francie would let loose a round of colorful verbal jabs, gaining power and momentum with each passing second. And although she loved her friend's fierce sense of loyalty, there was no point in their both losing jobs today.

Just as Francie was drawing a huge breath, Sydney walked over to her and placed her hands on her friend's shoulders. "It's okay," she said firmly, meeting Francie's gaze. "I'm not cut out for this anyway." She turned to Terwilliger. "I'll leave my uniform in the back."

She walked to the staff room, inhaling deeply to try to still the waves of anxiety crashing through her.

Great. Not only did she just let down her friend and ruin her first break at a job, she was back in the exact same predicament she had been in earlier. What was she going to do now? She had no experience, no connections, and no useful skills to speak of. Unless some amazing opportunity fell on her head, she had absolutely no leads.

Nope, Terwilliger was wrong. I definitely wasn't born to do this job. She took a big gulp of air as she pulled on her shirt and hung the wilted uniform on a white plastic hanger. *But was I born to do anything?*

3

"SYDNEY! HEY, BRISTOW! YOU can stop already!"

Todd de Rossi's husky voice rang out from the other side of the track, snapping Sydney from her thoughts. She slowed to a gradual stop and leaned over, resting her hands on her knees. "Did you say something, Todd?" she called breathlessly. Todd was on the men's track team, and sometimes their practices overlapped.

He raised his arm and pointed at his watch. "Women's practice was over ten minutes ago, just like men's," he shouted back. "I'm all for showing dedication, but I don't think your coach wants you to wear grooves in the running surface. Besides, don't you have classes today?"

"Yup." Sydney checked her metal-banded Bugs Bunny wristwatch. *Damn.* Her government seminar started in thirty-five minutes. This afternoon had flown by.

She'd really pushed herself today. Whenever she had something on her mind, running was the best way to purge the stress from her system. The rhythm of her footsteps and breathing always put her in a semi-hypnotized state, letting her sort through her thoughts and occasionally bringing about some clarity. But today she had a larger load than usual. After three-quarters of an hour, she was no closer to figuring out what to do about her job situation, and the wounds of the past couple of days were aching as much as ever.

She walked over to where Todd stood next to the bleachers, shaking out her legs as she approached. "I guess I just spaced."

Todd cocked his head at her, his darkly handsome features knitted with concern. "Is everything all right?"

Sydney stared at him, somewhat startled. Was she that obvious? She'd only known Todd a few weeks, so it didn't seem possible that he had her figured out yet. She studied Todd's face for a moment, wondering if she could confide in him. After all, she'd liked him from the start. Todd was one of those nutty theater/dance-major types, but he wasn't a phony. Sydney loved his deep, musical laugh, and the way his smile crinkled up his face, adding a starburst to his hazel eyes. But she didn't really know him. And Sydney didn't like moaning about her problems—even, sometimes, to Francie. It only made her feel weak.

"No. Everything's fine. Really," she said, flashing him a wide grin. "I just ate a whole pint of Ben & Jerry's last night and wanted to be sure and work it off."

"Oh, I hear you," he said, shaking his head sympathetically. "I love Chunky Monkey so much, my ex-boyfriend threatened to hold an intervention."

Sydney laughed.

"Anyway, I'm glad you're okay," he said, smiling warmly. "Well, I better hit the showers. See you tomorrow," he added, turning to head to the gaping steel door of the nearby locker rooms.

"See ya," Sydney called after him.

She walked around the track awhile, rotating her head and shoulders a few times. Then she stopped and stood on her right leg, holding the heel of her left sneaker against the back of her running shorts. Once she felt a warm tug down the front of her left thigh, she straightened up and repeated the move on the other leg.

You have got to snap out of it, Syd, she told herself, bending over and resting her hands on a patch of grass. *All this worry isn't helping, and you're starting to freak people out.* She pressed her forehead against her right knee, stood up straight, bent to the other knee. *Just push it out of your brain for a while. Relax. Enjoy the beautiful weather.*

She could feel her mood lightening a little as she took a deep breath and gazed around the track. It was one of those vivid cloudless days everyone took for granted in southern California. The sunlight was almost palpable, warming her body. On the other side of the chain-link fence, oak branches swayed in the light breeze. A mockingbird was chattering, hidden among the dense branches.

Why was she wasting time feeling sorry for herself? Sure, she had some heavy stuff to deal with. But maybe she should take some time to enjoy the beauty of the world around her.

Sydney gazed out at the fall foliage, waving her arms back and forth to loosen them up. All of a sudden, a flash of light caught her eye. Sydney squinted in the direction it came from. Parked cars lined the street. She remembered seeing one of them—a nondescript black sedan—when she had arrived at the track that morning. It was just the sort of car her father would drive: basic, drab, and sensible. Now that she looked more closely, she realized that the dark-tinted front passenger window was partially lowered, and the sun behind her was glinting off something inside the car. A pair of binoculars, maybe? Was someone sitting in there, watching her?

Sydney whirled around and marched toward the locker room. Any sense of calm that had come over her had instantly evaporated. It wasn't fair. She couldn't even have a good run without something bad happening. First the restaurant and now this. Was the world suddenly full of perverts?

* * *

Sydney propped her government textbook on its end to block out the scene in front of her.

"Open wide," cooed Francie from behind the book.

"Mmmm," came Baxter's deep murmur.

Sydney tried to concentrate on her reading. *Let's see.* . . . Democrats believed in social reform and internationalism. Republicans believed in a restricted government role, primarily in business and commerce. And Libertarians believed in—

"Crackers!" Baxter cried. "That's what we need." A series of kissing noises and indecipherable sounds followed.

Francie giggled slightly. "Aw, look. See what you made me do? Now you've got ranch dressing all over your mouth."

Sydney sighed in exasperation. It didn't bother her so much that Baxter was now joining them for lunch every day. He was cool enough. And his fun-with-food flirtfests with Francie really weren't the problem either. The problem was Sydney. She felt almost irrelevant. A useless lump with no life who had glommed on to Francie.

Francie could make friends with anyone. Whether she was standing in line at the grocery store, waiting at a city bus stop, or even sorting her unmentionables in the dorm laundry room, the girl could chat with strangers as if they were long-lost siblings. It was because of Francie that they'd met in the first place. Sydney, however, was shy. Not the kind of shy that implied she was scared of people—she just had a healthy respect for the space that separated individuals.

Some people misread her as being snotty just because she preferred to spend her breaks reading instead of gossiping. But it wasn't that she felt she was better than everyone. She just didn't feel the need to voice all of her opinions to everyone at any given moment. She had her long, giddy girl talks with Francie, and that was enough.

Wasn't it?

"Hey, Syd." Francie's head suddenly appeared over the top of Sydney's book as she stood up, Baxter following. "Want to go over to Westwood with us? There's a new coffee shop that has live jazz in the afternoons."

"I don't think so," Sydney replied, pushing the thought of a frothy cappuccino and a cool instrumental from her mind. "I've got a lot of studying to do for this test."

"You sure?" Francie asked.

"Really, Francie. I'm swamped," she said, gesturing to the books and papers spread out on the picnic table in front of her. "You guys go on."

"Okay," Francie said with a shrug. "Good luck with your exam. I'll see you back at the room."

"Bye, Syd," Baxter said, lifting his hand in a wave. Sydney noticed a small smudge of salad dressing on his upper lip.

Sydney watched them walk off hand in hand. For some reason she thought of Dean, and the old, familiar humiliation crept back into place.

She quickly looked away, pushed up the sleeves of her pale blue button-down, and bent back over her notes, trying to ignore the churning inside her.

"Excuse me. Ms. Bristow? Are you Sydney Bristow?"

Sydney glanced up. A man in a black suit had materialized next to her. He looked around fifty, with thinning reddish blond hair that was already almost halfway gray. His broad shoulders and chest suggested an athletic background, perhaps an ex-football player.

"Yes . . . I am. I'm Sydney Bristow," she said, momentarily taken aback. She wasn't used to having men approach her on campus, especially ones with such proud posture—or ones wearing such official-looking clothes.

"My name is Wilson. I'm a recruiter for the Central Intelligence Agency."

His face was blank as he handed her a gray business card. Sydney squinted down at it. The logo read *Credit Dauphine Bank and Trust*. Below that was the name *Reginald Wilson* along with an address and a phone number. There was no other information, and no mention of the CIA.

Sydney looked up into his face. Bright sunlight spilled on his shoulders. Was this some kind of fraternity stunt? "Really," she said, not bothering to hide the skepticism in her voice. "Didn't they do this gag already on one of those hidden-camera shows?"

"I assure you I'm not joking," he went on in his flat, unemotional voice. He reached into his breast pocket and pulled out a leather billfold. Then he flipped it open, revealing an identification card with an official CIA emblem at the top.

Sydney blinked. Maybe he was for real. Despite the warm afternoon, goose bumps tickled her arms. What could the CIA possibly want with her? Had she spoken up too much in government class? Forgotten to pay an old parking ticket? Stupid explanations barraged her brain.

The barest hint of a smile sneaked across Mr. Wilson's face as he pocketed his ID. "There's no reason to be alarmed," he said, as if reading her mind. "We are looking for worthy students to train for positions within the agency. We feel you would be a perfect candidate."

Sydney's mind capsized. "Me?" she asked, more breath than voice. "Work for the CIA?"

"If you decide you are interested, call the number on the card," he went on, paying no attention to her shocked expression. "And please don't lose it.

We aren't listed and we won't be approaching you again."

Sydney stared at him, then at the card, then back at him.

"But whatever you decide to do," he added, his voice becoming even more serious, "you must not tell anyone about this conversation—ever. I cannot stress that enough."

"Okay," she said feebly, a sense of panic brewing inside her. "I—I won't."

"Good," he said, the sternness disappearing from his voice. "I hope to hear from you soon." Then, with a nod good-bye, he abruptly turned and headed down the sidewalk.

Sydney's eyebrows scrunched as she watched him go. *As if they'd believe me anyway,* she thought in a trance, tucking the card safely into the front pocket of her backpack.

* * *

The next morning between classes, Sydney went to her special hideaway in the College Library in the Powell Library building. She'd scoped out a secluded back corner of the reference section during her first week at school. The spot was quiet and cozy, and Sydney felt at home among the big dusty volumes. This was where she went when she needed to do some serious studying—or thinking.

She sat on the hardwood floor, her feet propped against the side of the oak bookcase in front of her, her lap serving as a desk. She tucked a strand of hair that had escaped from her ponytail back behind her ear and frowned down at her biology textbook. She had a major exam that afternoon, and she was supposed to be reviewing the differences between plant and animal cells. Instead, all she could think about was the card in her backpack.

For the rest of the afternoon the day before and all through the night, she'd mentally reviewed her conversation with Reginald Wilson. He had seemed honest enough, and his ID appeared to be real, although she imagined that sort of thing could be faked. And yet when she came to the part where he said the CIA wanted to recruit her, her brain always shut down. The thought itself was just too slippery to grasp. Not only slippery—*bizarre*.

The *CIA* was interested in *her*? She'd sooner believe that she'd won the ten-million-dollar Publishers Clearing House prize, that Francie was becoming a nun, or that a spaceship full of aliens wanted to take her for a joyride.

A person who worked in top-level government

would have to be practically superhuman, wouldn't she? Strong and capable and afraid of absolutely nothing. *Not* a girl who got turned down flat for dates and couldn't even hold a waitressing job. The very idea warped her sense of reality. After all, if they would take her, they'd take anyone.

Forget about it, she told herself, lifting her textbook closer to her face. Obviously this was someone's idea of a joke. And right now, she really didn't need the stress. Wilson was probably just an actor some fraternity had hired to go around pulling pranks.

But what if he wasn't? said a voice in her head. Her eyes wandered back to her bag's front pocket. *What if he was real, and so was his offer?*

Sydney closed her textbook and reached for her backpack She unzipped the front compartment and pulled out Wilson's stiff gray card. The thing was, she *wanted* to call. She wanted it to be real. If he hadn't given her the card, it would have been much easier to dismiss the whole thing as a hoax. A product of her overactive imagination. But the card lent it credence, like a souvenir or an invitation— something small and tangible that brought new, exciting visions to her mind.

She sighed heavily and stared out the large

picture window at the far end of the room. The students outside were all moving along the sidewalk singly or in neat little clusters, their eyes focused, their strides steady and unwavering. Some were laughing; others were deep in thought. All of them seemed to know where they were going.

And what about me? Sydney asked herself. *Where am I going?*

It was becoming less and less clear whether her goal of becoming a teacher was the right choice. In fact, all her carefully laid plans were crumbling around her. She was earning perfect grades, but her classes weren't exactly filling her with a wild sense of purpose. The few people she had met only seemed interested in besting everyone else—and those who didn't were more interested in hooking up with each other than actually learning anything. Even she had to admit that the high point of her days was meeting Francie for lunch. Only now that Baxter was in the picture, she didn't feel like doing that, either. She was beginning to feel as if she didn't belong anywhere.

So here she was. Hiding in a dark corner of the library, burying herself in books.

It probably isn't a real offer anyway, she thought for the umpteenth time. Most likely if she called the number, she'd hear a group of jokester frat boys on the other end. She didn't need that kind of disappointment. And even if it was for real, she'd only be setting herself up for another probable failure.

Sydney closed her hand around the card and glanced over at a nearby trash bin. She sat for a moment, wondering what to do. Then she rose slightly and quickly tucked the card into her back pocket.

For some reason, she couldn't let go of it. At least, not yet.

4

"THOUSANDS OF ENGINEERING students on this campus are trying to figure out how to defy gravity, and my hair is doing it on its own!" Francie grumbled. She slid her freshly manicured fingers down the length of her thick black hair and frowned at her reflection. "You think one of them could come do research on me for their graduate thesis?"

Sydney sat watching from her bed, her long legs straight out in front of her, feet dangling over the edge. "Relax, Francie," she said, pursing her lips in an amused half-smile. "You look amazing."

Francie flashed her a grateful grin and then turned back toward the mirror over the built-in dresser. "I just don't want Baxter to think I've joined a punk rock group or something. A lot of his friends are going to this party and I don't want to embarrass him." She pulled her hair back, clasped it with a shiny metal clip, and then quickly yanked it out with a frustrated grunt.

"Here, let me," Sydney said, rising to her knees and beckoning to her friend.

"Thanks." Francie crossed the room and backed up against Sydney's bed, her grass hula skirt making soft swishing noises as she walked. "You know," she said, handing Sydney her hairbrush, "I really wish you'd go with us. It's Friday night, Syd." She hesitated. "I know that thing with Dean was a major blow, but you shouldn't let that stop you from having fun. He probably won't even be there. And if he is, we can get the guys to beat him up."

Hearing Dean's name, Sydney felt a lurch in her chest, as if all her vital organs were swimming upward to shield her heart. "It's not that," she lied, forcing her hands not to shake as she carefully tugged the brush through Francie's long dark locks. "I'm just not up for a party tonight. I'm really worn out."

Francie sighed loudly. "Is that really it? Honestly? Because I just don't think I could enjoy myself tonight if I knew you were upset."

Sydney bit her lip. She always prided herself on being able to shield her emotions, but for some reason, she always needed a little extra effort with Francie. "Scout's honor," she said, holding up two fingers. "You were right about my course load being too heavy. This week was a killer."

"Promise me next semester you'll cut back to something normal. Like fifteen hours tops?"

"I promise," Sydney said, glad to hear that Francie sounded convinced at last.

She knew her friend meant well, but there was absolutely no way she could go to the party tonight. For one thing, she'd never been good at these social-event schmooze-a-thons. She just couldn't shake the feeling of being sized up by tons of strangers long enough to relax and have fun. Hanging out in pairs or small groups was more her thing. Besides, tagging along on Francie's big date with Baxter would make her feel like an even bigger dork. And Francie would probably play the part of personal coach, urging her to do this, say that, flirt here, flirt there. Sydney would end up sabotaging their special evening and humiliating herself yet again.

And what if Dean is there with his coterie of admirers? Sydney cringed just thinking about it. *No way.*

"Okay, hold still for just a few more seconds," she said, keeping a firm grip on the strands of hair she'd twisted into place. With her free hand, she reached over and grabbed a couple of her own brass clips off her dresser. Then she fastened the hair in place and fluffed out the ends. "There," she said, patting Francie's shoulders. "You're gorgeous."

Francie turned toward the mirror and smiled. "Perfect! Thanks, Syd. You seriously rescued me."

Just then, a sharp rap sounded on the door. Francie wheeled toward Sydney, her eyes the size of compact discs. "He's here," she mouthed, bouncing on the toes of her sandals.

"I'll get it," Sydney said, stepping off the bed. "You sit and look casual."

"Okay," Francie said, settling into a chair and smoothing the straps of her flowered halter.

Sydney made a move toward the door.

"No! Wait a second," Francie called out in a loud whisper, making frantic waving motions with her hands. "I don't want to seem too eager." She circled her right hand slowly a few times, as if marking beats to a song, then said, "Okay. Go ahead."

Sydney opened the door to find Baxter clad in Bermuda shorts and a Hawaiian-print shirt, leaning against the doorframe in a semi-seductive pose.

"Oh, hey," he said, quickly straightening up. "Is Francie here?"

"I think so," Sydney replied, trying not to laugh. "Come in."

As they walked back into the room, Francie broke into a wide grin and leaped up from her chair as if a small explosive device had been detonated beneath it. Then she suddenly paused and leaned casually against Sydney's dresser. "Hey, Baxter," she said coyly.

"Hey, Francie. Whoa. You look . . ." He broke off, shaking his head.

Francie's smile gained extra wattage. "Thanks," she replied.

Sydney sighed softly, taking a step backward to fade into the surroundings. It was great to see Francie so excited and happy. But she couldn't help feeling a small pang of self-pity, too. Would something this cool ever happen to her?

"Well, uh, we should probably go," Baxter said, nodding toward the door.

"Right," Francie said, shouldering her purse.

She turned to look at Sydney. "You sure you'll be all right here?" she asked worriedly.

"I'll be *fine*," Sydney said emphatically. "Besides," she said with a wink, "it'll be nice to have the room to myself for a while."

"Okay, then. Bye, Syd," Francie called as she and Baxter stepped into the hall.

"Bye, guys," Sydney said with a wave. "Have fun."

The door shut and Sydney sank down on the edge of her bed with a sigh.

Suddenly everything was quiet—almost *too* quiet. Any noise she could discern seemed amplified a thousand times. Each tick of Francie's Looney Tunes wall clock was like a tiny explosion. And for the very first time, Sydney could hear the high-pitched whine of their mini refrigerator.

For some reason, the usual dormitory racket was absent. There were no footsteps in the corridor or competing muffled melodies from distant stereos. Was there no one else in the entire building?

Probably not, she thought. She stood and took long, dragging steps to her desk, dropping into the wooden chair. *It's Friday night in L.A., for Pete's sake. Everyone else is probably out having fun or away visiting family for the weekend.* Everyone else had a life.

She had books.

Once again, a wave of self-pity washed over her, but she took a deep, steadying breath and forced it back down. Then she reached for her Spanish textbook, opened it, and tried to lose herself in a *historia* about a *niña* named Carmen. She had just gotten to the part where Carmen's *perro* ran away when she shut the book with a thunderous slam.

Forget it. She was not going to study tonight. So what if she didn't have a big date or a family waiting to greet her with hugs and a home-cooked meal? She deserved some fun, right?

Sydney jumped up and walked to her dresser, deciding to throw on some comfortable sweats and watch a video on the tiny TV/VCR combo she and Francie had splurged on at the start of the semester. As she pulled off her jeans, something small and gray fluttered out of the back pocket. Mr. Wilson's business card lay at her feet.

Sydney picked it up and studied it. The stiff paper stock was already soft and frayed from being handled so much. For the rest of that day after she left the library, she'd been almost hyperaware of its being in her pocket, as if it were somehow calling to her or giving off heat. She had pulled it out dozens of times during her afternoon classes, turning it over and over in her hands and restarting the debate in her head.

She stood frozen for a moment, wondering what to do. She could stick the business card in a drawer. Or maybe even her scrapbook? *Remember this?* she'd laugh to herself as she turned the pages. *The sunny September day the CIA tried to recruit me.*

No, she thought, crumpling it in her fist. It had been enough of a distraction already. Things were mixed-up enough without all these silly daydreams about working for an intelligence agency. If she didn't get rid of the thing, she'd drive herself crazy.

Sydney lifted her hand and launched the card into the air. It arced gracefully, landing in the wastebasket.

"There," she said, exhaling. "Now I never have to see it again."

* * *

Four hours later she was clad in her favorite blue sweats, leaning against the side of her bed with a bag of microwave popcorn balanced on her lap. On the tiny fifteen-inch TV screen, a stoic, gray-bearded Obi-Wan Kenobi was surrendering to Darth Vader, allowing Luke, Leia, Han Solo, and the droids time to blast their way to the *Millennium Falcon* and escape.

She could hear the faint scratching noises of a key in the lock behind her. A second later, the door opened and Francie stepped into the room. Her face was flushed and the clips in her hair had slipped slightly. Otherwise, she sported the same blissed-out expression she had had on her face when she left.

"Hey," Sydney greeted her, turning down the volume with the remote. "How was it?"

"Oh, you know parties," Francie said casually, trying to erase the grin from her face and failing miserably. "It was okay. The band sucked and I think some of the guests were in a contest to see who could be most obnoxious."

"But you had a good time with Baxter, right?"

Francie paused. "Yeah," she said softly, smiling off into the distance. "I did."

"Good," Sydney said, beaming back at her.

Francie threw her purse onto her bed and walked up next to Sydney, staring at the TV screen. "Oh, my god. I haven't seen this in like ten years. Why did you pull this out?"

Sydney shrugged. "Because, like you said, I hadn't seen it in a while."

She didn't want to tell her that almost every other movie in their paltry video collection was just way too depressing to watch during the pity binge she was currently on. She hadn't realized their assortment of films was such a downer until that evening. Scorsese's *Taxi Driver,* Coppola's first two *Godfather* films, Tarantino's *Reservoir Dogs,* and the few Hitchcock classics they owned were just too gory or angst-ridden. And after the Dean incident, she didn't think she could handle the Julia Roberts romantic comedies. So she opted for pure sci-fi action.

"Did you watch this first?" Francie asked, holding up the copy of *Raiders of the Lost Ark* Sydney had tossed onto her bed.

"Yeah."

"You always did have a thing for Harrison Ford, huh?"

"Yeah."

Francie hiked up her hula skirt and sat down cross-legged next to Sydney, who passed her the popcorn. For a while, they sat watching the film silently.

"You know what I don't get," Francie said through a mouthful of popcorn.

"What?"

"At the end here, Princess Leia gives these huge medals of valor to Luke and Han and even Chewie, right?"

"Right."

"Well, how come that other fighter pilot doesn't get one? What's his name? Wedge? I mean, he totally saves Luke's butt a couple of times but then has to pull out when his ship gets too damaged. But flyboy Han swoops in at the last second to help after being a total putz and *he* gets an award. What gives?"

"I don't know, Francie," Sydney said with a chuckle.

"It just bugs me. That's all."

"Maybe they can make another movie where he gets back at them for that," Sydney suggested, bumping her shoulder against Francie's.

"Yeah. *Star Wars Twelve: Wedge's Revenge.*" Francie held up her hand, gesturing to an invisible theater marquee. "He's back! He's mad! He wants his medal!"

Sydney slumped forward, laughing. "Stop! You're going to make me choke!"

Slowly, their giggles subsided and they lapsed back into their silent viewing. Sydney glanced at

Francie's profile and smiled. She remembered all the hundreds of times she'd imagined what college would be like, hoping she'd have a nice roommate to share things with. Now here she was, in college with a terrific roommate. One who already had romance and excitement. Sydney had . . . videos.

Without warning, hot tears suddenly surged into Sydney's eyes. She stared up at the ceiling, trying to will them back into their ducts. She knew if she blinked, they'd start running down her face, growing into a steady trickle. *Stupid,* she scolded herself. *Watching* Star Wars *and crying for no reason.* But she couldn't help it. It was as if something had pounded a crack into the invisible protective coating surrounding her. Swift as rushing water, the crack spread and divided, destroying the armor and leaving her raw feelings exposed.

She blinked. A current of tears ran down her cheeks. She clapped her hand onto her mouth, trying to hold back a sob, but that only made it worse. A muffled cry died in her throat, but the force caused her to lurch forward.

Francie looked over. "Syd?" she said in alarm. "Honey, what's wrong?"

Sydney could only shake her head, blinking rapidly, trying desperately to stop the waterfall of tears.

Francie hit the mute button and scooted up beside her. "What is it?" she demanded.

"I'm just . . . I'm just tired," she croaked, wiping her face with her hands. "I shouldn't have stayed up this late."

"Come on. Tell me the truth." Francie leaned closer and wrapped her left arm around Sydney, trying to stare up into her face. "What's really going on?" she asked softly.

The concern in her friend's voice seemed to dissolve whatever strength Sydney had left. She gave up fighting the emotions storming inside her and crumpled against Francie's shoulder, sobbing loudly.

For a few minutes Francie simply patted her left arm and rocked her softly, murmuring, "Shhh. It's okay," over and over. Finally, when Sydney's crying subsided, she pulled back and peered into her eyes. "Please, tell me what this is about," she said, her forehead creased with worry. "I really want to help."

Sydney took a long, shuddering breath, feeling simultaneously ashamed, pathetic, and completely worn out. "I'm just so . . . lost," she began, staring down at her hands. "I've been a total failure at everything lately."

"Hey," Francie whispered, squeezing Sydney's

wrist. "That is so not true. I know you've had a bad couple of days with the whole Dean thing and the jerk at the restaurant, but—"

"No. It's not just that." Sydney sighed slowly. She leaned back and shut her eyes, wading through her cluttered thoughts and emotions. "I really thought college would be this huge open door to a new life. But it's not. The professors aren't these superwise mentors; they're just people. Most of the students I've met are just as phony as the ones in high school. I thought I'd feel so free and powerful. Instead I just feel really . . . disconnected." She opened her eyes and stared wearily at Francie. "If it weren't for you, there'd be nothing for me here."

Francie grabbed Sydney's hand in both of hers, clasping it tightly. "Listen to me," she said, her voice simultaneously firm and soothing. "You are *not* a failure. You are beautiful and athletic and supersmart. So what if you haven't found your thing yet. You will. You just need to believe that."

Sydney lowered her eyes from Francie's ultraresolute gaze. "I don't know. I hope so," she mumbled, staring down at her lap.

"I swear to god, girl, if you don't start believing how special you are, I'm going to start a petition. You know I would!"

Sydney laughed softly.

"I mean it!" Francie went on, waving her hands dramatically. "You know me. You know how picky I am, right?"

"Right."

"I don't see a movie unless some respectable reviewer gives it at least four stars. I don't eat most fast food, and I try not to wear clothes more than one season. Let's face it. I'm a snob." She nudged Sydney's ribs. "Come on, say it."

"You're a snob."

"So I ask you," she went on, her eyes round and watery, "would I choose just anyone to be my roommate?"

"Oh, Fran," Sydney said almost inaudibly, leaning sideways until her head was resting on Francie's shoulder. "Thanks for putting up with me."

*   *   *

Sydney awoke the next morning feeling achy and groggy. All night long she'd been plagued with strange, murky dreams of running away from something. What it was, though, she'd never found out. A few times she had opened her eyes, sat up to stare at the clock on her dresser, and immediately begun thinking about the card lying in the wastepaper basket. She was beginning to feel haunted by the thing.

A beam of sunlight shone through the window, cutting a bright stripe across the room's industrial-carpeted floor. Sydney pulled back the covers, slid out of bed, and padded over to the basket. The small metallic trash can seemed to glow. Leaning forward, she could still see one of the card's gray corners poking out from under a few Post-It notes. She reached automatically, hovering over the basket. Maybe she should at least call? The work of a government agent could be really interesting. Exciting even.

Yeah, well, it's too bad I'm really not the right type, she told herself, pulling back her arm. She really had to shake this from her mind before she freaked out entirely. What she needed was a long, brisk run.

As quietly as she could, she slipped into a clean set of sweats, pulled on her running shoes, and tiptoed past Francie's bed. Outside, the campus was ablaze with a vivid rosy light. The air was crisp, and except for her, the only things stirring were birds. Everyone else was probably sleeping off the lingering effects of a wild Friday night. *Oh well,* she thought. *At least I'll have the track to myself.*

But five minutes later, when she walked through the main gate to the athletic fields, she could see a lone figure stretching out at the side of the bleachers. "Todd?" she called as she approached.

Todd lifted his head and grinned. Then he quickly hopped to his feet and jogged over to her. "Sydney! Hey, doll. What are you doing here so early on a Saturday?"

"I was about to ask you the same thing."

"I guess I might as well tell you," he said, springing giddily on his Nikes. "I got some fabulous news yesterday and I've been bouncing around like a Super Ball ever since. I couldn't even sleep. I had to come out here and work all this energy off before I hurt someone."

"Well, tell me already," Sydney said, laughing. "What is it?"

Todd paused dramatically, glancing to either side of them as if there might be teams of reporters waiting with microphones. Then he clapped his hands together and blurted out, "I got cast in a gum commercial yesterday!"

"You did? Todd, that's fantastic!"

"Yeah, I know," he said, prancing up and down

the track like a football player celebrating in the end zone. "I got the call yesterday afternoon and I haven't been able to calm down since. Come on, run with me."

Sydney did a couple of quick stretches and then set off side by side with Todd. "That really is amazing," she said, lengthening her stride slightly to keep up with him. "When did you audition?"

"Monday."

"Oh, man. Have you been waiting by the phone all week?"

Todd snorted. "Are you kidding? No way. I figured I blew it."

"Really?" Sydney asked. "Why?"

"Because it was only like the twentieth audition I'd been on since I moved to L.A. this summer. And every call I've gotten has been Thanks, but no thanks. Of course, those were the people who actually called back. Lots of them don't even bother."

Sydney shook her head. "That is so rude."

"I was really starting to doubt myself," he said, making a face at her. "I even started thinking about switching my major from theater to marketing. But I'm so glad I hung in there. *This* is what I'm supposed to do," he declared, stretching his arms out to the sides. "Today, gum. Tomorrow, toothpaste!"

Something suddenly clicked in Sydney's mind.

She slowed to a stop, Todd's words echoing through her head like a siren's wail. *That's it,* she thought. Her crazy stress, the lure of the card . . . All this time she'd just been scared. The Dean and Les Amis disasters had left her completely rattled, too afraid to take another chance. But if she kept on shying away from opportunities, she'd never find out where she belonged.

"Sydney?" Todd called from several yards down the track. "Are you coming?"

She glanced up, blinking her present surroundings back into view. "No," she shouted. "I just . . . I just forgot something important."

"What?" He cocked his head curiously.

Sydney began walking backward, her brain whirling with activity. It felt as if she were waking up for the second time that day. "Sorry, Todd. I've got to go," she called. "I'll see you tomorrow at practice." Then she turned and ran out the main gate, heading straight for the dorm.

* * *

"Surprise!" Francie cried as Sydney burst through the door, red-faced and dripping with sweat. "I cleaned up!"

"Huh?" Sydney pushed a few long brown

strands out of her face and glanced around the room. Sure enough, everything was freshly picked up and dusted. Francie had even made both beds.

"I'm sorry I've been such a slob lately," Francie went on. "I know I've been totally preoccupied with Baxter and all, and here you are with your super-brain schedule doing all the chores and wearing yourself out. Well, that's going to change. I swear from now on, I'm going to be the world's best room-mate. Well, no. That's you. Okay, I'll be the world's *second*-best roommate."

Sydney snapped out of her daze and headed straight for the wastepaper basket. It was empty.

She spun around and stared at Francie, her eyes wide with alarm. "What did you do with the trash?"

Francie looked confused. "I took it out," she said slowly, watching Sydney with a baffled expression. "I threw it in the Dumpster out back. It's a good thing, too. I could hear the garbage truck a few streets over. He must be on his way."

Sydney gasped. A dense heaviness crowded into her gut. The card! If she lost it, she'd never get to call the agency back! Wilson had made it very clear that they wouldn't contact her again.

In a flash she was running out the door and down the hall, halfway conscious of Francie calling after her. She burst through the door to the stairwell and started flying down the steps, pushing past several bleary-eyed students. At the bottom, she raced through the front lobby and burst through the double glass doors to the street outside. Cars were pulling up to the front curb, full of people coming for weekend visits. Sydney veered around a group of people hugging, vaulted over a bicycle rack, and sped around the corner to the back of the building.

There, in the narrow back alley, stood the large metal Dumpster. She exhaled in relief as she spied a black garbage bag poking up over the rim. It was still full. And yet somewhere in the distance she could hear the hollow clangs of a Dumpster being emptied. The truck would be here any minute.

I have to find that card, she thought. *No matter what.*

Her mind a blur, Sydney leaped onto a stack of crates, tossed back one of the lids, and threw her legs over the side of the Dumpster. Inside, it was dim and the temperature seemed twenty degrees higher than the air outside. A sickly sweet smell of rotting food filled the air. She walked around in a slow circle, looking downward, her tennis shoes squishing against the unsteady strata of trash bags.

"Let's see, it would have to be near the top," she

mumbled to herself, her sharp brown eyes darting around wildly. "A white bag. Maybe halfway full." Unfortunately, she was ankle-deep in white bags.

All of a sudden, the roar of a large diesel engine snapped her from her thoughts. She peered over the edge and saw the garbage truck blocking the other end of the alley. There came a loud squeaking and hissing of brakes. A second later, the high-pitched tones of the rear-movement beeper started up.

In a panic, Sydney began lifting up white sacks and frantically examining them, searching for anything recognizable. All the while, the noise of the truck grew louder and louder. Her heart was pounding so hard, she could feel the throbbing down the length of her arms. And yet her mind remained strangely focused, unable to break from its task.

Just then, something familiar caught her eye. She snatched up a bag and noticed a bright, circuslike design through the thin white plastic. The empty popcorn bag from last night! This had to be it!

By now, the sides of the Dumpster were vibrating from the noise of the approaching truck. Clutching the trash bag tightly in her left hand, she threw her legs over the rim of the Dumpster and landed sprawled on the broken asphalt below.

Then she rolled against the back wall of the building and sat up, just in time to see the robotic arms of the garbage truck clamp onto the Dumpster and raise it off the ground.

"You are *nuts*," she said to herself as the Dumpster clanged against the bed of the truck. Its contents slid out and landed with a series of sickening plops.

Hopefully, it had been worth it. Her palms still stinging from their impact with the ground, she fumbled with the knot at the top of the bag and opened it. Sure enough, the wadded-up business card was lying just beneath the popcorn bag.

Sydney leaned back against the cinder-block wall and sighed with relief.

* * *

Monday morning after track practice and a shower, Sydney stood pacing in front of the row of back-to-back pay phones along the sidewalk by her dorm. Her pulse was racing and something large and heavy was pressing down on her chest. She hadn't felt this way since she was eight years old and was attempting to go off the high dive for the first time.

What are you waiting for? she asked herself,

fiddling with the silver heart pendant on her necklace. *It's business hours on a weekday. Prime time. Just take a deep breath and dive. . . .*

She walked to the nearest phone, picked it up, and entered her calling card number. Cradling the receiver against her shoulder, she held up the battered business card and carefully punched in the right series of digits. Her hands were trembling and her breath came out in short gasps. Almost immediately, the other end picked up.

"This is Wilson," a voice said curtly.

"Uh . . . Mr. Wilson? This is Sydney Bristow. You, um, gave me your card a few days ago on the UCLA campus?" She tried to sound confident, but instead the words tumbled out airy and shrill.

"Yes, Sydney. Let's not talk on the phone. Come to the Credit Dauphine building this afternoon after your Spanish class." He gave her directions, which Sydney scribbled on the back of her English notebook. "Just give the card and your name to the woman at the front desk and ask for me."

"All right." Then Sydney frowned down at the receiver. "Wait. How do you know my schedule so well?"

But there was no reply. Wilson had already hung up.

To: bossman@creditdauphine.com
From: reginald.wilson@creditdauphine.com
Subject: Sydney A. Bristow

You were right. She called.

To: reginald.wilson@creditdauphine.com
From: bossman@creditdauphine.com
Subject: Sydney A. Bristow

Good work. Continue preparations.

5

ON MONDAY AFTERNOON SYDNEY pushed through the front doors of the Credit Dauphine bank building in downtown Los Angeles and was immediately awash in noise. She stood in the polished stone lobby, listening to the ringing phones, the whirring of unseen machines, and the steady undercurrent of voices. People rushed to and fro in front of her, most of them clad in neutral-colored business suits, many of them talking into cell phones.

She glanced down at her Gap khakis and

multicolored striped sweater, feeling conspicu-
ously young. What was she doing here? She didn't
belong in a place like this. What if they took one
look at her and decided they'd made a gigantic
mistake? For a brief moment, she thought about
leaving. But she knew if she didn't follow this
through, she would forever wonder what she had
missed.

She smoothed the back of her hair, making certain her tortoiseshell clip was still in place, and
walked over to the high, oval-shaped front desk.
Behind it a woman with a sleek blond bun sat talking on the phone. After a moment, she hung up and
regarded Sydney, flashing her a tight, overly polite
smile. "May I help you?"

Sydney stepped forward and placed the worn
business card on the wooden counter. "My name is
Sydney Bristow. I'm supposed to meet with a Mr.
Wilson."

The woman's smile disappeared and her eyes
quickly scanned the room. "Please come with me,"
she said in a low voice.

Sydney followed the woman through the vast
lobby to an elevator, which they rode down to a
long, navy blue carpeted hallway. They reached an
unmarked door.

"Have a seat inside. They'll be with you in just

a moment," she said to Sydney, then turned and vanished back down the corridor.

They? Sydney thought as she opened the door and stepped inside. The room was sparsely furnished but extremely bright, thanks to glaring fluorescent lights and a large window overlooking the lobby. A giant wooden desk sat in the center of the room. Behind it, six executive-style leather chairs were arranged in a semicircle. One plain, wood-framed chair with gray fabric cushions faced the desk. *Must be my seat,* Sydney decided, lowering herself into it.

A thick manila file lay in the middle of the desk. Craning her neck, she could read her full name lettered across the front. *Is that for me?* she wondered. *Or* about *me?* Listening for any approaching footsteps, she reached across the desk and pulled the folder toward her. For a moment she sat staring down at it, biting her thumbnail. The temptation was too strong. *It couldn't hurt to just take a peek,* she decided. Taking a deep breath, she grabbed the bottom corner of the cover and flipped it open.

And there she was. Clipped to the top of the inside cover was a photo of her eating salad at the campus picnic tables. Right underneath was another of her running around the track. She felt a churning sensation in her gut. Why did they take these? And when? The photographs were crisp and close up, but she'd never noticed anyone snapping pictures of her.

A stack of papers lay bound inside the file. Her eyes widened as she scanned the pages, each crammed with details about her life. There were copies of her birth certificate from the West Virginia hospital where she was born, her Social Security card, her driver's license, medical records, school schedule, grades, test scores, even copies of her dental X rays.

Sydney slowly let out her breath. "My god," she murmured. "They've got everything but my fingerprints." As she spoke, she turned another page, and there, blown up to several times their normal size, were her finger- and thumbprints. "Oh, my god," she repeated, more loudly. She couldn't imagine how they had gotten them. She wasn't sure if she even wanted to.

A realization was slowly seeping over her like wet cement, making her stiffen in her chair. *This is for real,* she told herself. *These guys are the real deal.* She knew she should probably shut the folder and try to relax, but she couldn't. There was something morbidly fascinating about seeing her-self broken down into words and pictures.

As she rummaged toward the back of the folder, she was shocked to find her own handwriting in the pile. It was a photocopy of a letter she'd sent to Melissa, an old boarding school friend, over the summer, complaining about her father and describing how eager she was for college to start.

The CIA had somehow intercepted her personal mail. She swallowed, trying to ignore the spin her brain was in. How long had they been watching her, anyway?

A typed note clipped to the back read:

```
Handwriting sample 1-B.
Graphology analysis reveals strong
independent streak, generosity,
high originality, theatrical skills,
insecurity, cautionary approach
toward people, and high need for
solitude.
```

All of a sudden, a noise from behind made her jump. Footsteps were reverberating down the corridor, several pairs by the sound of it. Her pulse hammering in her ears, Sydney quickly closed the folder, slid it back to the other side of the desk, and sat back in her chair.

Less than a second later, the door opened and Wilson stepped inside, followed by four stony-faced men and one woman wearing a drab burgundy coatdress. All carried yellow notepads.

"Hello again, Sydney," Wilson greeted her as he and the others filed around the back of the desk. "I hope you haven't been waiting too long."

"No, not at all," Sydney replied, trying to smooth her features into a casual smile.

Wilson sat down in one of the chairs. The others followed suit. "I've asked my colleagues here to join us during the interview," he said, gesturing to the clones on either side of him. "For security reasons I cannot introduce them to you by name, except to say that they are here to represent the agency's top-tier personnel. You understand."

"Of course," she said, trying to mask her irritation. *So it's okay for them to know me down to my bra size, but I can't even have their first names? How fair is that?*

Wilson glanced around the room. "All right. If everyone is ready, why don't we get started?"

Burgundy Coatdress lifted her pen to get Sydney's attention. "Miss Bristow, could you describe the emotional state you are presently in?"

Sydney stared into the distance, pondering. What *wasn't* she feeling right now? She was simultaneously scared, scandalized, and completely amazed. She felt nervous, yet incredibly curious, too. And even though she was intimidated enough to try to remain polite, she'd also let go of that standard job-interview urge to present herself as being better than she really was. Let them see the *real* person they'd spent valuable time and tax dollars profiling. The person the file barely revealed.

"Let me rephrase the question," she said. "Do you trust us?"

"No," Sydney said plainly. She'd expected there to be lots of frowns and exchanged glances, but everyone seemed perfectly fine with her reply.

"What are your feelings toward the United States Government?"

Sydney shrugged slightly. "I don't always agree with it, but I'm loyal to it."

"Can you explain?"

"Even if some of the government's decisions don't seem right to me, I have to assume they know more about the situation than I do, so I shouldn't question it." She wondered how politically correct that statement was. Did it matter?

This immediately caused a torrent of note-taking, even a few nods as they wrote.

For the next twenty minutes the five nameless suits quizzed her on a barrage of different topics—

school, athletics, her favorite books and historical fig-
ures, hobbies, diet, and sleep schedule. Meanwhile,
Wilson sat watching silently, never taking a single
note.

Sydney answered everything as truthfully as
she could, and yet she couldn't stop thinking about
the dossier on the table and all the secrets inside.
What exactly did these people want from her?
What were they hoping to discover?

"Miss Bristow, can you tell us what types of
music you enjoy?" asked the man in the navy blue
suit.

Sydney laughed. "I don't know. Lots of stuff,"
she said, shaking her head in astonishment. "Does
it really matter?"

The man continued to stare at her blankly. "It
matters. Could you give us some examples of what
you like to listen to?"

"Oookay," she said, fidgeting with the hem of
her sweater. "Let's see . . . everything from alt rock
to trash new wave and Euro-disco. I listen to classi-
cal while studying. But I go more fast-tempo when
I work out. Lately I've been running to this guy my
roommate really likes, Raul Sandoval. I guess you'd
describe his music as Latin hip-hop meets hard-
rock power guitar."

She rubbed her eyes as five pens simultaneously scratched against paper. How much longer was this going to go on? The questions were starting to become even stranger.

"Miss Bristow, have you ever broken the law?" asked the woman.

"No," Sydney replied, taken aback.

"Have you ever wanted to?"

"No," she repeated incredulously.

"Have you ever admired a criminal?" asked a man in a red paisley-print tie. "Or a particular crime?"

"No!" she said again. Where were they going with this?

A man in black pinstripes lifted his hand. "Miss Bristow, are you in a relationship at the moment?" he asked.

"Excuse me?"

"Can you describe to us the current state of your love life?" he clarified, sounding slightly huffy.

Sydney stared into his face, anger welling up inside her. "I don't have one," she said finally.

She sat fuming as they quickly made note of this. She hoped this would all be over soon. The questions were getting more and more personal, and they were beginning to dredge up several unwanted emotions. Plus, she couldn't quite shake the notion that she was being put on trial for something.

"Miss Bristow?" The gruff-looking man in gunmetal gray sat forward in his chair. "Could you please describe your relationship with your father?"

Sydney pursed her lips, a new surge of anger jetting up from within. "I really don't see what my father has to do with any of this."

"It has a lot to do with *you,* Miss Bristow. Now could you please answer the question."

"No! That's it," she said, shaking her head. "I've been really patient and cooperative with all of these questions, but you haven't told me anything about you or what you want me to do."

Mr. Gray Suit's expression hardened slightly. "All you have to do is tell us—"

"That's all right." Mr. Wilson held up his hand. "If Sydney doesn't want to answer the question, she doesn't have to. I think we have all the information we need." He rose from his chair and the others stood as well. "Now, unless there are any objections, I believe Sydney is ready for the next phase of the interview?"

He glanced around at each of the suits. No one said a word.

"Fine. Thank you all for your assistance," he said with a dismissive nod. One by one the others filed from the room, shutting the door behind them. Wilson walked over and lowered the blinds on the window. Then he took a step toward her, a somber expression weighing down his features. "Sydney, what I'm about to show you can't be talked about beyond this building. To do so would bring serious repercussions."

"I understand," she replied, the firestorm in her stomach making her hunch slightly.

"I need to know if you are willing to go farther," he said, icy eyes boring into hers, "or if you want to leave and never come back."

Sydney fought the urge to chew her thumbnail as she considered his words. Clearly she should not take today's events lightly. And yet, for some reason, she was beginning to feel a sense of trust and respect toward Wilson. He really seemed to have a lot of confidence in her, and she liked the way he took her seriously and didn't talk down to her—the way her father always did.

She really hadn't expected to come this far. In fact, she'd halfway assumed the interview would end with them realizing they'd made a horrible mistake. But obviously she'd passed the test, at least for now. She really wanted to see how far she could go. Plus, any misgivings she had were being doused by an overwhelming curiosity.

"I'm in," she said emphatically.

Wilson stared at her for a moment and then nodded. "Good," he said. He walked over to the desk and reached underneath the tabletop. Suddenly, a panel in the side wall slid sideways, revealing a gaping doorway.

"Welcome, Sydney," he said, gesturing to the opening, "to CIA covert ops."

* * *

Sydney stepped over the threshold and blinked hard. She was now in a vast, windowless space, filled with rows of people wearing headphones as they sat in front of giant computers. Each terminal had at least four screens and a dizzying array of buttons, dials, and light-bar displays.

The room throbbed with activity. Even the air seemed electric. The steady hum of machinery was punctuated by voices shouting out combinations of words and numbers, none of which made any sense to Sydney. She couldn't believe she'd been on the other side of the wall for almost an hour and yet never heard a single noise.

"You are now entering our training and tracking area," Wilson said. He pressed a keypad on the wall beside him and the wall closed itself up again. "Our headquarters are located elsewhere."

He strolled down one of the aisles and Sydney fell into step after him, her mind whirring along with the room's equipment. "So . . . the bank upstairs. They know you're here, right?" she asked.

"Basically we are the bank," he replied. "To the outside world, it's a completely legitimate financial institution. And yet it also allows us to heavily safeguard this building with no questions asked. What you are looking at now is our state-of-the-art surveillance system, which is vital to our intelligence-gathering operations." He swept his hand through the air as he walked, gesturing at the assortment of people and gadgets.

Sydney nodded as he talked, trying to look as if she comprehended everything.

"Follow me," Wilson said, heading for a glass door at the back of the surveillance room. "Let me show you the rest of the compound."

There's more? Sydney wondered, following him through the door. *Right. Of course there's more.* Walls with hidden panels . . . a bank that housed a top-secret security force . . . a file detailing her every move, compiled without her knowledge . . . She had fallen into a dazed, Alice-in-Wonderland-type stupor and would probably have been only slightly surprised to see giant caterpillars sitting on toadstools or a talking cat that could make itself invisible. *But what am I doing here?* she asked herself over and over. *Why did they come to me?*

The rest of the compound was just as stark and windowless as the training room. Wilson showed her a file room, a soundproofed firing range, and a large area divided into cubicles with computers, which he simply referred to as the "testing room." There were also several doors they passed that they did not enter. Sydney could only imagine what secrets they held.

"It takes people with all kinds of skills to run this organization," Wilson was saying as they turned yet another corner. The compound layout was a dizzying maze of twisting corridors and rooms that led to other rooms. Sydney had already abandoned the notion of finding the way out on her own—but then she doubted Wilson would ever leave her side.

"Last of all," he said, gesturing toward a large glass partition, "we have our combat training center."

Sydney stepped forward and peered through the window. Inside was a barren studio with a large, padded mat in the middle of the floor. On it stood two men, facing each other in taut, partially crouched stances. One was older, with gray hair and a thick salt-and-pepper mustache. The other looked to be in his mid-twenties, with a thatch of brown waves.

"Yoav used to work as a combat trainer for the Israeli military," said Wilson from behind her. "Right now he's instructing one of our agents in the Krav Maga fighting method. This is not your smooth, artistic type of martial arts. It's all-out, no-holds-barred street fighting. The type of thing we're most likely to face in the field."

Sydney leaned even closer, fixing her eyes on the younger guy. He was amazingly cute. Not the slightly spoiled, nonchalant good looks of Dean, though. This guy was older and more rugged, and from what she could tell, in incredible shape, too. As she studied the fierce, focused way he jabbed and dodged his opponent, she sensed a certain magnetic intensity. She found herself wondering about him. What was his name? Where did he come from? What sort of life did he lead before this?

All of a sudden, the young man's eyes shifted toward the window. Sydney drew back slightly and sucked in her breath. She could feel her face redden as her heart started up its own martial arts routine. Their gazes locked for less than a second and then . . . *Wham!* In one swift move the older man lunged forward and tossed the younger guy onto the mat.

"Let's move on," Wilson said, continuing down the hallway and rounding another corner.

Sydney pulled her gaze away from the cute guy's sprawled form and walked after Wilson. *Snap out of it, Syd,* she scolded herself, giving her head a small shake. What a ditz. She saw one hunky guy and immediately turned into a drooling mess—*not* a good way to impress a potential boss.

Wilson led her farther down the passage, through an unmarked door, and into yet another meagerly furnished office. "Please have a seat," he said, shutting the door.

She settled into the chair facing the desk and tried hard to appear casual—as if she got glimpses into covert law enforcement organizations every day of the week. Wilson lowered himself into his seat and stared at her. He seemed to be trying to read her thoughts, and she looked back at him without actually meeting his gaze, focusing instead on the tiny wrinkles beneath his eyes and the scattering of freckles across the bridge of his nose.

Eventually he leaned back, resting his clasped hands on his stomach. "I've now shown you everything I can allow at this point," he said, twisting his chair back and forth. "Do you have any questions?"

"Hundreds," she replied. "But mainly . . ." She paused and pursed her lips, then quickly launched the question that had been plaguing her for days. *"Why me?"*

Wilson's red-blond eyebrows flew upward. "Can you not see yourself working for us?"

She exhaled slowly. "I don't know. You've shown me lots of stuff, but you haven't really told me what I'd be doing. Would it be a desk job, some kind of research help? Or something . . . else?"

"Let me explain," he said, leaning forward and resting his hands on the desktop. "Our agency is always in need of new recruits, but we have to be extremely careful who we bring inside. We need people who are smart, athletic, alert, and able to think on their feet. You've shown all of these qualities. You demonstrate the perfect profile of someone who could be a first-rate undercover operative."

Sydney held her breath as a small tremor rattled her insides. So they really did want her to be a secret agent. *Her*. It was too unreal. On the one hand, she felt incredibly flattered and excited. But on another level, she was just very, very scared.

"Like all new recruits, you would begin at a desk job," Wilson continued, "slowly immersing yourself in the organization and learning about our operations. Then after a while, you would start your transition to becoming an agent, taking on intense physical and weapons training. The entire process takes approximately two to three years."

For a moment, Sydney could only smile in disbelief. Then she shook her head. "But what if . . . I mean, what happens when . . . How can you be sure you have the right person?"

For the first time since she had met him, Wilson flashed her a genuine grin. "All right, look. Beyond your genius-level IQ, beyond your speed on the track, and beyond your talent for linguistics, I've noticed that you have this keen sense of justice. Remember that goon at Les Amis?"

Alarm bells went off in Sydney's head and a flood of pictures came rushing back. "You . . . you were there!" she exclaimed, pointing at him. "You were sitting at the bar. You were wearing a goatee and tie-dyed T-shirt, but it was you! Wait a minute." Her mind spun up a fresh set of images. "Were you the one sitting in the black sedan by the track field?"

Wilson nodded. "See? You have excellent powers of observation. Just the sort of thing we need." Then, as quickly as it had appeared, his smile suddenly faded, replaced by a piercing stare. "These are the terms of the offer, Sydney. You have twenty-four hours to consider this position. If you want the job, I must hear from you before five P.M. tomorrow. You can tell no one the truth about what we do here. All your friends and family will know is that you've been offered a position as an office assistant in a bank. You will be given a complete briefing as to how to handle all inquiries regarding your position with us."

For some bizarre reason, Sydney had relished the opportunity to tell her father about this amazing turn of events. *See, Dad? You don't want me—but Uncle Sam sure does!* She hadn't really planned on doing it. But the fantasy had been soothing nonetheless.

"And if I decide not to take it?"

"You still mustn't tell anyone. I cannot stress this point enough. Lives depend on our maintaining the utmost secrecy. Any breach of confidence is handled severely. We exact the ultimate price on those who do not abide by our rules."

Death? Was he saying she would be killed if she told anyone what had transpired? Did the CIA do that? *I won't try to find out.* She nodded mutely.

"Well then," Wilson said, returning to his casual monotone. "I'll show you out now." They rose from their chairs and headed for the door. "And Sydney?"

"Yes?"

"I hope you take the job."

6

THE CIA WANTS ME! The CIA wants me! Sydney practically danced up the stairs of her dorm. The same thought had been tolling in her head since she had left the bank building, like some sort of mini opera. *She* could be a secret agent. A spy! If she wanted to, that was. Still, even if she decided not to go through with it, it was exciting to know they believed in her.

She pushed through the door to her floor and half-skipped to her room.

"Where have you been?" Francie shrieked

when Sydney walked through the door. "I've been so worried!"

Here goes, Sydney told herself. She smiled at Francie and tried to remember the phrases she'd rehearsed between mental musical numbers. "I was at a job interview," she said.

"What?" Francie's eyes popped open wide. "Where?"

"At this bank downtown," she replied, sitting on the edge of her bed and pulling off her shoes. "They offered me a job as a clerical assistant. No big deal."

"'No big deal?'" Francie repeated incredulously. "Are you crazy? This is great for you! I mean, aren't you going to take it?"

Sydney couldn't help grinning. "Maybe," she said truthfully. "I mean, it's a bank job. I'm not exactly sure I'm cut out for it."

"Hey, it's got to beat fetching soup for rude weirdos. I'm so proud of you!" Francie ran over and shook Sydney's shoulders excitedly. "You know what we need to do? We need to go out and celebrate."

"I don't know," Sydney said, hoping she didn't look suspicious. Going out for a night on the town wasn't what she had in mind. She could imagine the quandry she'd be in, sitting in a neon-lit bar with her friends. *Hmmm, I'll be thinking. Should I*

become an undercover agent for the CIA— Oh,
excuse me, waitress, more nachos and another
round of margaritas, please! Now where was I?

"Come on!" Francie urged. "We can make it a
group thing. I'll call up Baxter, and you can invite
that mental friend of yours from the track team.
What's his name? Todd?" She kneeled down and
grasped Sydney's wrists. "You know, you haven't let
yourself go crazy since we got to college. This is a really cool thing. You deserve to live it up a bit."

Sydney looked into Francie's eyes. She'd kept
things from friends before. Like . . . like not telling
Melissa that her dress for the ninth-grade formal (a
vision in magenta silk) was hideous. Or . . . or the
fact that she hated carrot cake, the year Caitlin, her
boarding school roommate, couldn't be there for
her birthday and had ordered one from the bakery
down the street as a surprise. Or that the guy
Francie had had a crush on the summer before was
seen holding hands with Francie's worst enemy.
Granted, becoming a superoperative for the CIA
was a *teeny* bit of a bigger deal, but . . .

Who was she trying to kid? This was the
hugest deal she had ever faced, that she could have
dreamed of facing. Nothing this exciting had ever
happened to her before. In fact, things like this
hardly ever happened to *anybody*. It wouldn't hurt

to go out for a short while—to let her friends help her celebrate. Then she could come home and figure out her life.

* * *

An hour later Sydney was sitting at a corner table in a large, smoky club near the Santa Monica Pier. Across from her, Francie and Baxter sat cuddled together, and on her left, Todd lay back in his chair with his arms folded across his middle and his long legs stretched out in front of him.

"This band wants to be U2 so bad, and it is just *not* happening," Todd said over the music.

"Really?" Sydney asked. "What's wrong with them? I think they sound okay."

"It's the attitude," Todd said, raising his hands in a big, theatrical gesture. "All rock musicians today are supposed to ooze anger. What do four prelaw students from Burbank have to be angry about?"

"Okay. What is up with all this angst-ridden music these days?" Francie shouted from across the table. "I mean, what's so bad about happy, dancey tunes?" Baxter leaned close and whispered something in her ear, making her giggle.

Todd shook his head in mock pity. "Poor

Francine. Didn't you get the memo? People don't dance anymore. They just pose." He sat up straight and lifted his chin, a haughty scowl creasing his features. Everyone laughed.

"Well, I don't care what anyone says," Francie said, rising to her feet. "I'm going to bounce around the floor like Snoopy." She reached down and grabbed Baxter's right hand. "Come on, let's go do a happy dance."

"I'm in," Todd said, leaping from his seat and offering his arm to Sydney. "Will you join me, milady?"

"Sure."

The four of them walked out onto the empty dance floor and started moving to the music. At first, Sydney had a tough time ignoring the stares inevitably drawn by people who danced when no one else was dancing. She hung back slightly and swayed back and forth, laughing at the others' flamboyant moves. Todd, Francie, and Baxter were purposely overdoing it, shaking their bodies and thrashing their arms as if they were contestants in an MTV dance contest. Eventually, Sydney began to get into the spirit and was surprised at how good it felt. She shut her eyes and let herself go, swirling her arms and gyrating her hips while her friends egged her on.

"Go Sydney, go Sydney, go Sydney!" they chanted.

It was like running track, only louder and more hyper. All of the stress that had been weighing her down lifted from her shoulders and took flight. Francie had been right about her needing this. She couldn't remember the last time she'd had this much fun.

The song ended and the four of them fell against one another, laughing.

"Come on, Todd," Baxter said, nodding toward the bar. "Let's go get these divas some Cokes."

Laughing and panting, Sydney and Francie walked unsteadily back to the table and sat down.

"See? You can blow off your work or studies once in a while and it won't kill you," Francie said breathlessly as she patted down her tousled hair. "Besides, it's not like you're on some major deadline. Right?"

It was as if someone had slapped Sydney in the face. She blinked around her, and the rest of the world came zooming back into focus. The giddiness left. And the decision she'd been ignoring stepped back into her conscience.

She glanced down at her watch. It was already after ten o'clock. Wilson said she had only twenty-four hours to consider the job. If she wanted time to really think about the offer, she should get back to the quiet of their dorm room.

"Sydney?" Francie said impatiently. "What's up? Do you want to leave?"

"What? Oh, well . . . yeah, actually," she replied, scrunching her nose. "Do you mind? I've really got a lot to do."

"This job thing really has you confused, huh?"

Sydney opened her mouth to say something, then quickly shut it, shrugging instead.

"I know you haven't asked my advice, but so what. I'm giving it anyway." Francie inched her chair up next to Sydney and placed a hand on her forearm. "I know you, Syd, and I have to ask: Is it possible you're overthinking this?"

Again, Sydney shrugged. She appreciated Francie's concern. But she was also afraid that if she opened her mouth, she might accidentally say too much.

"I mean, it's just a *job*," Francie continued. "It doesn't have to be the start of a lifelong career. And even if it is, what's so wrong about working in a bank? We can't all save the world, you know."

Sydney stared at her friend in alarm. In her preoccupied state, it took her a while to realize

Francie had only been using an expression. "Yeah. I know," she said finally.

"Anyway, that's all I'm going to say," Francie said, leaning back in her chair. "If you want, we can leave right after the drinks. Okay?"

Sydney didn't reply. Her mind was still reeling with Francie's words. *Is that it?* she wondered. *Am I making a big deal out of something that is really very simple?*

The thing was, she actually *did* have the chance to help save the world. In that sense, the job was perfect. So the real question had to be was she right for the job?

*   *   *

Sydney lay curled on her bed, facing the wall. After dropping her off, Baxter and Francie had gone on to a café in Santa Monica, so she had the entire room to herself. There was no sound at all—except for the residual ringing in her ears from the club's loud music. She finally had all the solitude and quiet she needed to think things through. Only it wasn't turning out to be the peaceful meditation she'd hoped for. Instead, she felt dizzy and confused, as if a fraction of her were still twirling on the dance floor.

So far she knew this much: She wanted the job.

She really did. And yet a nagging insecurity kept nibbling away at her enthusiasm. It was as if she were about to go skydiving. She felt eager and excited, but she also knew that if she didn't pack her parachute just right, she'd be in for a long, painful fall.

Just like her plans to become a teacher. For so long she'd taken for granted that it was her dream to follow in her mother's footsteps. And it hurt to discover she might not be cut out for it. Not only because she was left without a clear path, but also because it might mean she was less like her mother . . . and more like her father.

Her father was definitely *not* the save-the-world type. The man sold airplane parts for a living; he was a total square. In fact, he wasn't even as dimensional as a square. He was more like a line—plain, rigid, narrow in scope, and running directly away from her.

Sydney closed her eyes and conjured a mental image of her dad. His broad, inexpressive face, sharp features, and weary-looking eyes. Handsome yet lifeless. The sort of person everyone respected, but no one liked.

Even she didn't like him much. And yet, on another, more subconscious level, she knew that she loved him. For years she had craved his approval, clinging to the hope that they could someday forge a closer relationship. She had thought they could get to know each other as adults once she'd gone on to college. She just hadn't yet found the nerve to try.

"What about now?" she mumbled, sitting up. She could use a dad right now. Other people had normal relationships with their fathers and could call on them for advice. Why not her? Of course, she couldn't exactly tell him what was on her mind. And it would be a modern-day miracle if he listened. But maybe there was some way she could get guidance from him without actually revealing her problem.

She reached over and snatched her phone off the desk. Then she hit his speed-dial number and waited, her fingers doing a nervous drumroll on the receiver.

After four rings, someone picked up. "This is Bristow," came her father's gruff voice.

"Dad? It's me, Sydney."

"Sydney? It's after eleven. Are you in some sort of trouble?"

"No, I'm fine. I just . . . wanted to talk." She winced at how young and meek she sounded. Why not ask him for a drink of water and a bedtime story while she was at it?

"Talk? About what?"

She shrugged. "Anything, really. How's work?"

"Demanding," he blurted out irritably. "In fact, I've got an important meeting at eight o'clock in the morning. Why are you really calling?"

"Jeez! Can't I call up my dad and see how he's doing?" she shrieked, jumping to her feet. "Why don't you even ask me how *I* am?"

"Because it's late and I have to get up early. I imagine you do too." She heard the staticky sound of his sighing into the receiver. "Look, Sydney, I don't have time for this. I know you need money, so why don't you just come out and say so instead of going through this whole routine?"

Sydney's jaw dropped and she slowly sank down onto the edge of her bed. "You think I just called you for money?" she mumbled, her eyes filling with tears. "Is that what you think? Well, you're wrong," she went on, her voice rising angrily. Any earlier fantasies she'd had of telling her dad about the CIA vanished. "You can keep your cash. In fact, I just called to tell you that I have a job now, so from now on I won't be needing *anything* from you!" Before he could reply, she turned off the phone and threw it onto the bed behind her.

That's it, she thought, wiping a tear from her cheek. *I am definitely taking the job.*

No way was she going to end up like him. A man who cared more about selling jet engines than talking with his own daughter! She, on the other hand, had a chance to make a difference in the world, and she'd be crazy not to take it.

She could only imagine how proud her mother would be.

Good morning, Mr. Wilson. After careful consider-
ation, I want to let you know that **I'm in.** I, Sydney
A. Bristow, would like to become an official agent
of the U.S. Government and enter the employment
of the Central Intelligence Agency.

Uncomfortable silence. Nervous titter. Pass out
and crumple to the floor.

No matter how many times I practice saying those
words, it doesn't seem any more real. Not yesterday. Not this morning. And not, I imagine, when I
report to Wilson's office at the Credit Dauphine
bank building in downtown Los Angeles later this
afternoon to tell him I have decided to take him up
on his offer. To become a **superoperative agent**
and undergo amazing missions and have training
up the wazoo. Or whatever it is I'll be doing.

You know why I decided to accept the CIA's offer?
Because the more I think about it (and believe you
me, all I have been doing for the past twenty-four
hours is thinking. Pondering. Ruminating. Screaming.), the more I have come to realize that it is
an **incredible opportunity**. In-cred-i-ble. How
many people in their lifetimes have the chance

to do something really important? Something for their country, something truly meaningful and life-changing? Using my powers of observation to gauge happiness at my local food mart, not many, that's for sure. Take my dad. Selling airplane parts. Sure, people have to fly, but is his vocation truly significant? Can wheeling and dealing in jet engines be fulfilling to anyone?

I can't say I'm not scared. I am. Wilson wasn't kidding around, I know that. Death. He implied that I could be **killed** for telling anyone what I now know. He doesn't know, though, that I already have experienced death. Had my legs kicked out from under me, my heart yanked through my throat and stomped on with an indescribable ferocity, my world shattered into a zillion tiny pieces that no one helped me put back together.

Then again, considering who we're talking about, maybe Wilson does know that. That would mean he knows that after facing that, I can handle anything.

Or die trying.

SIX MONTHS LATER

7

SYDNEY HUNCHED OVER THE desk, her forehead resting against her fingertips. To her left, a stack of files towered over her, each stamped CONFIDENTIAL in bright red block letters. In front of her, spread over the entire surface of the desktop, was an array of maps. They looked like normal road maps except for the numbered red dots scattered across their surfaces, each corresponding to a file photo and a page or two of written detail.

She shook her head slowly and let out a long, low whistle. Never again would she be able to see the world as one gigantic travel brochure. According to the maps, hidden below postcard-perfect German pastureland were dozens of nuclear missiles. A major weapons arsenal was stashed behind a crumbling Spanish church. And just half a mile from a popular Venezuelan beach stood a suspected chemical weapons plant.

Reaching into the nearby file, Sydney pulled out the map marked *North America* and gingerly unfolded it. She immediately sucked in her breath. The red dots were everywhere—it looked as if the paper had measles. Was there no safe place left on earth?

"I work for the CIA," she murmured as she carefully refolded the maps and replaced them in the folder. "I work for the CIA."

It was her mantra, her hymn. She'd started the chant months ago, when the enormity of what she was doing for a living hadn't quite sunk in yet. After she had accepted Wilson's offer, there had been a whirlwind of activity.

"Don't worry, we'll have you out of here in time for your English class," Wilson had told her on that long-ago—was it just last autumn?—day. "We still have several hoops for you to jump through before it's a done deal. You'll need a complete physical and psych evaluation, plus a battery of intelligence tests, and you'll need to sign about two dozen nondisclosure agreements." She had been adamant about continuing her studies at UCLA. "That's perfectly fine," Wilson had assured her. "In fact, we wouldn't have it any other way. You'll still need a cover for your friends and family. It would be completely out of character for you to drop out of school to accept a clerical position at a bank, wouldn't it?"

She had nodded, vaguely uneasy at how well Wilson seemed to know her "character."

Wilson had opened the door of his office and motioned her into the corridor. "In the meantime, there's no reason why I can't show you where you'll be reporting for duty."

As she walked alongside Wilson, Sydney had felt a swelling sensation inside her chest. This was it. Her new life was officially starting! She wondered where this "duty" would take place. Maybe the martial arts room? Or the artillery range?

But instead of leading her into the hidden compound, Wilson had brought her back out into the bank lobby. He walked up to the same blond receptionist she'd approached the day before and said something in a low voice to her. At once, the woman walked around to the front of the counter and stood beside him, smiling at Sydney.

"This is Maxine," Wilson explained. "You will report to her each time you come into work."

"But . . . what about you?" Sydney felt silly asking, but somehow, she'd grown almost fond of Wilson over the past few days. She didn't like being passed on to someone else.

"Oh, I'll be around," he replied, giving her a rare all-out grin. "Remember what I told you. We'll be watching you very closely, and we'll let you know when we think it's time for you to"—he paused and glanced around at the people in the lobby—"move up."

"Come with me, Sydney," Maxine said, beckoning with a finger.

Sydney followed Maxine into a nearby elevator. As the doors closed, she stole a quick glance at Wilson. He nodded at her as if to say, "You'll be all right." Then the doors slid shut and the elevator began to rise.

Sydney's knees jiggled nervously. She looked at Maxine out of the corner of her eye, taking in her perfectly cut suit and shiny blond hair. She couldn't help wondering what her story was. In fact, she couldn't help wondering about every person in the place. What sorts of things did they do for the agency? How much did they know? Were they happy?

A moment later, the elevator halted on the twentieth floor. The doors slid open and Maxine exited, gesturing Sydney to follow. They were now in a long, carpeted hallway with offices staggered on either side. Sydney could hear the steady chugging sound of a photocopier, and phones rang from all directions like crickets on a clear night. A woman bustled past, balancing a stack of paper and a steaming cup of coffee in her hands. Then a man crossed the hall, staring down at an open file as he walked.

Maxine led her into a dimly lit room with tall black file cabinets running along both walls. "Here we are," she announced, turning up the buzzing fluorescent lights with a dimmer switch. "This is where you'll be spending most of your time. When you first arrive, you will pull files according to this order board and deliver them to people around the building. During your rounds you will pick up materials they have to return, bring them back here, and refile them."

"Okay," Sydney said, trying to look motivated.

Maxine smiled at her. "I know it isn't the world's most exciting work, but it's a good way to learn your way around. After a while you'll start doing more challenging things like researching cases and writing reports."

"How long does it usually take before . . . ?" Sydney paused, unsure how to phrase her thoughts, and unsure whether she should say them out loud. After everything Wilson had told her, and after watching how cautiously he had spoken in the lobby, Sydney was terrified of letting something slip out at the wrong place or time.

"Before your transition?" Maxine asked, tilting her head.

Sydney's eyes widened. Okay. So apparently they *could* talk freely here on the twentieth floor.

"Usually about two years," Maxine continued. "Sometimes people are moved up sooner, though."

"I see."

"Well then," Maxine began, clapping her hands together. "If you have another moment to spare, I'll show you how to work the Xerox machine."

"Great," Sydney said, mustering up as much enthusiasm as she could.

So much for playing Emma Peel, she thought, falling into step behind Maxine.

Then, after several weeks of making copies and delivering files, she started being asked to summarize case documents and collect information on particular subjects. Sydney read mountains of data, a heady blur of photos and reports that she absorbed into her photographic memory like a sponge soaks up water. And a brand-new world opened up to her—a world full of lurking dangers.

Instead of being filled with fear at these discoveries, Sydney had become impatient to do whatever she could to help. "I work for the CIA," she would whisper during her morning shower, her drives to work, her solitary jogs. So full of mad pride at what she was a part of, she felt she would explode if she couldn't tell anyone.

So she told herself.

"Sydney?" Maxine's head appeared in the doorway now, her gold bracelet clinking against the frame. "Do you have that paper on radio surveillance finished?"

"Yes. Right here," Sydney replied, opening her top left-hand drawer and pulling out a stapled document as thick as a paperback romance. "And I have that report on South American mercenaries, too," she added, snatching up another set of papers.

"Already?" Maxine exclaimed, stepping into the room. She grabbed the documents and began looking them over as if they were rare and valuable artifacts. "I don't know how you churn these things out so fast. It's as if you can breathe this stuff in and out. What are you? Superhuman?" She shot Sydney a wide, gleaming grin and then turned to go. "Don't forget to distribute those memos," she called over her shoulder.

Sydney shook her head. *Superhuman?* Maxine was constantly raving about Sydney's fantastic writing skills and ability to beat deadlines. At times, Sydney wondered if *Maxine* might be more than human. She looked more like a top-secret cyber-creation than a real person, with her permanent smile and perfect outfits. In fact, Sydney wouldn't have been surprised to discover the Mattel logo stamped across her backside.

But Maxine was right about Sydney's almost inhaling her assignments. Everything she came across seemed so important and fascinating. And the more she learned, the more restless she became for more. It was as if she couldn't get enough.

Sydney stood and stretched her arms. Then she picked up a stack of papers off a shelf near the copier and headed down the hall, placing one sheet in each of the mailboxes mounted beside every door.

"Sydney?" called a deep male voice behind

her. Sydney whirled around to see Wilson's hefty frame filling the hallway.

"Uh . . . hi," she said, completely surprised. She'd barely seen Wilson since she'd started working for Maxine. "What's up?"

"It's time, Sydney," he said. "Come with me." His expression was as blank as usual, but something in the way he looked at her suggested a smile.

Time? Sydney's pulse accelerated. "Sure," she said, grinning nervously. "I'm almost finished with these—"

"Leave them here." He cut her off, taking the stack of memos from her hands and placing it on a nearby table. He headed toward the elevator, nodding for her to follow.

Wilson gave no hint of what was to come as they rode down, leaving Sydney to her own thoughts. *Is it finally happening?* she wondered. *Am I going to start my agent training?*

No way, came another voice from inside her. *It's only been six months and everyone says it takes at least two years. They probably just want to throw some harder office work your way.*

Eventually the elevator slowed to a stop. They stepped out into the lobby and followed the path to Wilson's office. As they walked in, two people immediately rose from their seats along the wall.

"This is Yoav," Wilson said, indicating a large, muscular man with a thick mustache. "You might remember him from our first tour. He trains all our agents in hand-to-hand combat."

"Yes. Hi," Sydney greeted him.

The man bowed slightly.

"And this," Wilson continued, pointing to a tall, proud-looking woman with dark eyes and an abundance of long black hair, "is Pilar. She is one of our top weapons specialists."

"Hello," Sydney said, smiling at the woman.

The woman nodded and smiled back.

"Please sit down," Wilson said, waving toward the empty seats. Sydney sat, along with the two instructors. Wilson lowered himself into his chair and stared directly at Sydney. "I'll get right to the point," he began. "The people at headquarters feel it's time for you to begin your transition to becoming an agent."

A floating feeling came over her. Sydney felt as if she were expanding upward, becoming at once taller and lighter. *I was right,* she said to herself. *Somehow, I made it.*

Wilson looked at her expectantly, waiting for a response. Gripping the arms of her chair tightly to prevent herself from rising to the ceiling, she inhaled deeply. "Great. Thanks. Only . . . what does that mean exactly?"

Wilson, Yoav, and Pilar exchanged brief glances. "It means no more pushing paper on the twentieth floor," Wilson replied. He reached over and handed her a small plastic card with a series of letters and numbers printed across it. "Here is the code for the keypad that activates this wall panel. I want you to memorize it and give it back before you leave today. Beginning tomorrow when you arrive for work, you will come through here and report directly to Pilar at the firing range. After your lesson with her, you will report to Yoav for your combat training. Following that, you will get a brief shower and break before you report to me. I will oversee your covert ops training."

Sydney listened attentively, her head swiveling in a semicircular motion. It was all happening so fast. This was what she'd been dreaming about for months, and now that it was finally coming true, it seemed completely surreal. She squeezed the card in her fist, letting it dig into her palm. She needed to feel something real, something aside from this heady daze.

"It is important that you keep up the appearance of working as a bank clerk," Wilson went on.

"You should continue to dress formally and change into workout clothes here."

"All right," she said, still smiling and nodding. "Thanks."

"Congratulations, Sydney," he concluded, leaning across his desk to shake her hand. "We've never had anyone move up this quickly. You've already demonstrated an amazing understanding of our work, and the people down in headquarters want you on the fast track."

"The fast track," she repeated, swallowing. She had believed that she was doing a good job, but this formal recognition was somewhat overwhelming. "Thanks," she said again, at a loss for words.

"I guess my only question is," Wilson added, gripping her hand firmly, "do *you* think you're ready, Sydney? Are you ready to become an agent?"

8

"HIIAAH!"

Sydney whirled around and struck the man with her elbow.

"Reeeaah!"

He countered with a slicing side kick.

Sydney leaped to the side, rolled, and sprang back to her feet, turning to face her instructor once more. Her senses were on ultra-high alert. Every muscle in her body felt taut, as if she were a cobra poised to strike. There was no studio, no mat, no sweat running down her back and chest. All she could see was Yoav's tall, brawny form looming in front of her.

She watched him closely, ready to react at any sign of movement or shift in balance, searching for a weakness she could take advantage of.

With barely a trace of motion in his upper body, Yoav suddenly swung his leg around in a side kick. Sydney immediately jumped up and out of harm's way without taking a single second to decide.

"Excellent," Yoav said, still in his prowling stance. "Let your instincts take over. Shut down your logical mind and trust your reflexes."

Sydney allowed a flash of a memory to seep in. Her first sparring session with Yoav after weeks of training with pads and punching bags. She'd been too intent on impressing him, too focused on what her next move might be rather than what was happening at the moment. *I'd been concentrating too hard on specific moves. Yoav showed me to spread my focus much wider. To focus on unbounded energy.*

It had taken a while to learn how to silence the analytical side of her brain, which was typically in high gear. But once she had, the experience was exhilarating.

Yoav's shoulders swiveled almost imperceptibly, and without thinking, Sydney knew what his next move would be. Sure enough, his body twisted to the right, his left elbow swinging upward and out. In a flash, Sydney simultaneously ducked the blow and threw her fist into his exposed side.

Yoav stumbled forward. "Good!" he exclaimed, wheeling around again. "Next time, don't ease up on me. Really let me have it." His eyes challenged her. "We've got medics in the building if anything happens."

Sydney gave a brisk nod as she tried to stay in her zone. She knew she was restraining herself. The thing was, even though she was getting good at dodging and disarming, when it came to landing real blows, she could feel herself pull back a little. Her mind still couldn't quite accept it as real.

Yoav stalked sideways a few steps, moving in front of the large viewing window. As Sydney studied his posture, something in the distance caught her eye. Almost mechanically, her gaze shifted toward the glass. There, in the corridor outside, stood the guy she'd seen during her first tour of the compound. He was staring right at her, his rugged features softened by a crooked grin.

It's him, her mind shouted. She'd been thinking about him for months, wanting to ask Wilson or even Yoav about him, but too afraid she might reveal herself as a silly, crushing teenager. And now here he was. Watching her.

Sydney felt her pulse quicken and then all of a sudden, the whole world turned upside down. For a fraction of a second she was flying backward through the air. Then she landed with a jarring thud on the mat. She lay there, gasping, staring in bewilderment at the coiled bulbs of the overhead lights.

Yoav's face loomed, his bushy mustache framing his downturned mouth. "A distraction in the gym can cost you a sore body. A distraction in the field can cost you your life." He held out his hand and pulled her to her feet. "Never let yourself get distracted."

"I'm sorry," she said, sucking in air. She couldn't help herself. She quickly glanced toward the window.

The guy was gone. The corridor was empty.

A wave of disappointment washed through her.

"That's all for today," Yoav said, grabbing a dingy white towel off a hook and tossing it to her. "Wilson said he needed to see you early today, and that you should go straight to his office. No time to shower."

"Okay," she said, pressing the towel to her forehead and neck. "And . . . um, sorry about letting my guard down just now," she added, feeling sheepish. "I saw . . . movement, through the window. It just sidetracked me."

He peered at her closely, his thick brows so low, they practically blocked his eyes from view. "You *should* notice all things, Sydney. Be aware of your surroundings, but stay focused. There's a difference between watching and wondering."

"Duly noted," she said, nodding. "I better go. See you tomorrow." Draping the towel around her shoulders, Sydney pushed open the heavy steel door of the studio and stepped out into the corridor.

She had just turned the corner and was heading toward Wilson's office when she saw him. The guy was standing with a couple of older, blue-suited men, scanning an open notebook. She slowed down slightly, a sudden burst of cardiac activity hindering all other movement.

Just then, he glanced up and smiled at her. Sydney swallowed. Her feet and fingers gradually became numb as all her blood rushed into her cheeks. She lifted a corner of the towel and swiped at her face, acutely aware of her red, blotchy skin, droopy ponytail, and sweat-streaked tank top and sweatpants. Why, of all days, did Wilson have to override her shower this afternoon?

The guy nodded at her, and Sydney nodded back, her mouth automatically lifting in a smile. *Damn, he's cute.* She briefly flirted with the notion of walking right up to him and introducing herself. But three steps into her deliberation she'd already completely passed him. Doing a total about-face in the hall would be embarrassingly obvious.

She only hoped her backside wasn't quite as bad as her front—in case he was looking.

*   *   *

Her heartbeat had decelerated somewhat by the time she reached Wilson's door. Sydney knocked three times and entered.

"Hi, Sydney," Wilson said, glancing up from the mosaic of photos and papers on his desk. "Thanks for coming early today. Sorry to rush you like this. I've got a really important meeting later and have to make things fast."

"No problem," she said, taking her usual seat at the smaller desk that faced his.

Memories of past misery rumbled inside her.

She'd heard that "important meeting" excuse from her dad on an almost weekly basis while growing up. The difference was that he had never bothered to apologize. He'd always made it clear that work came first, and any disappointment she might have suffered was simply collateral damage.

Sydney opened the bottom drawer of her desk. Inside lay a stash of notebooks and manuals.

"Take out your manual on nonverbal communication," Wilson instructed as he rose from his chair. He pressed a button on his desk keypad and a white screen automatically lowered from the ceiling. "I hope you did some studying."

"Yes," she said, making a face. "But I'm still confused. I just don't see how analyzing posture or counting eye blinks helps with covert ops."

"It helps a great deal. Recognizing someone behaving out of the ordinary is usually your first clue that something dangerous is going on. And keeping your own actions as natural as possible will allow you to remain undetected in an undercover situation."

That should be easy for me, Sydney thought with a wry smile. Most of her life she'd been good at moving in and out of places without being conspicuous. That way she avoided having to deal with people unless she truly had to. Unfortunately, being so anonymous also made her invisible to the

Dean Carotherses of the world. When she wanted to get noticed, she usually wasn't.

So then why did the cute agent smile at me? she wondered, her grin spreading across her face. *What does he see when he looks at me?*

"The main thing is to blend into the environment as best as you can," Wilson continued, snapping her back to the present. "Dress the same way other people dress. Drive what they drive. Move and talk the way they do. Do as little as possible to call attention to yourself. Now." He pressed a hand-held remote and a picture of a crowded street flashed onto the screen. "Somewhere in this photo is a known terrorist. Can you spot him?"

Sydney bit her lip. "The man in the gray jacket," she replied.

"Good." Wilson nodded approvingly. "What made you choose him?"

"Because judging from the foliage and the rest of the people's clothing, the weather is warm. That could mean he's wearing the large jacket to hide some sort of weapon."

"Excellent. What are some other clues to look out for?"

Sydney's gaze traveled upward as she thought. "Stiff upper-body movement, an immobile hand kept out of sight, unusual bulges or lumps in their attire."

"Correct. There are right ways and wrong ways to conceal a weapon on your body, which I'm sure you've been learning. How is your weapons training going, by the way? Pilar told me you were eight of ten in the black."

Sydney smiled. "Yeah. But on the pop-ups I always—"

Just then, the phone on Wilson's desk started ringing. "Excuse me," he said, lifting the receiver. "This is Wilson. . . . Yes. . . . Tell Sloane I've got the dossiers. I sent down the surveillance data this morning. . . . Yes, I got the message. Five o'clock . . ."

Sydney absently flipped through the manual, not wanting to look as if she was listening. She'd heard the name Sloane before while passing through the corridors. She had no idea who he was, but judging by the hushed tones people used, she figured he was really important.

"Yes. Tell Sloane I know he'll be pleased. . . . He wants what? I see. Excuse me a moment. Sydney?" Wilson said, covering the mouthpiece with his free hand. "This might be a while. Would you mind taking your manual out into the corridor and doing some reading while I finish?"

"Uh . . . no. No. Not at all," she said, trying not to appear curious. Wilson had never asked her to leave during a conversation before.

Sydney grabbed her book and stepped out into the busy hallway. She felt instantly conspicuous, like a student who had been too disruptive in class. Being banished out of hearing range was a blatant reminder of how out of the loop she was.

Oh, well, she thought. *Might as well do what the teacher said.* She slid down the wall into a cross-legged position and thumbed through the manual. A chapter heading caught her eye: "Body Language and Feelings of Intimacy." This was one of the sections they had passed over, but it sounded a lot more interesting than some of the stuff they'd been studying. She quickly skimmed the paragraph headings and diagrams.

"Frequent touching is typically a sign of emotional attachment, or an interest in forming one," began one section. *"These touches are typically more direct yet gentle and are focused on more personal areas of the body, such as the face or hands."*

Duh, Sydney thought, turning the page. How many research dollars had been wasted figuring that out?

A photograph on the opposite page caught

her eye. It showed a young, dark-haired Dean Carothers clone leaning against a wooden fence. A girl was standing next to him in obvious flirt formation. Her body was contoured to meet the curve of his slouched stance, her head was tilted coyly to the side, and her hands were clasped around his left wrist, lifting it so she could (supposedly) check the time on his wristwatch.

Sydney scowled at the picture, her brow creasing into a pattern of wavy lines. She had never been able to do that stuff. In fact, it amazed her how expertly some girls could throw themselves at guys. She shut the book and stared at the opposite wall, trying to imagine herself using body-language methodology on the nameless agent. "Hi, I'm Sydney," she could say, strolling right up to him and grabbing his forearm. "Do you happen to have the time?"

Forget it, she thought, erasing the mental image with a shake of her head. *There's no way I could pull that off without feeling like a total dork.*

Wilson's voice suddenly broke through her thoughts. "Come back inside, Sydney," he said, leaning into the hall. Sydney quickly jumped to her feet and stepped into the room. "I'm afraid our lesson is going to be extra short today," he added, shutting the door and striding quickly back to his desk. "I've got to be at headquarters in ten minutes."

Ten minutes? Sydney wondered, her curiosity surging once again. If he could be there in ten minutes, headquarters couldn't be very far. Maybe it was located in another downtown building . . . but which one?

"That's all right," she said, placing the book on body language back in the drawer. "I guess I'll see you tomorrow afternoon then." She turned to go.

"Just a moment." Wilson held up a hand. "Before you leave, there's something I need to give you." He reached into his top drawer and pulled out something small and square. "A pager," he explained, handing it out to her. "So that we'll always be able to contact you."

Sydney took the sleek black box from his grasp. *This is major,* she thought as she slowly turned it over in her palms. *They must really trust me.* A warm, cozy feeling slowly seeped over her. "Thanks," she said in a hoarse whisper.

"Go ahead and start wearing it all the time," Wilson said, an odd expression knitting his typically inert features. "You never know when we might be needing you."

9

"YOU MADE IT!" FRANCIE'S dazzling smile shone like a beacon through the Lion's Den, a smoky, cellar-like jazz club not far from campus.

"Hey! Am I late?" Sydney called as she made her way to the table and dropped into a roughly hewn wooden chair. She set down her purse and tugged on the bodice of her dusty blue tank dress. She'd finally ended up getting her shower right before leaving to meet Francie. But in her hurry, she had neglected to dry off well, and now the water on her body was gluing her outfit to her skin.

"Nope. I was early." Francie groaned. "You would not believe the day I had. First I discover I studied the wrong two chapters for my sociology quiz. Then I go to work and find a busload of tourists in the restaurant demanding to know where all the movie stars are. Finally they leave and I go up to this skater dude who's paying for his smoothie, and he pulls out these dollar bills from—I'm totally serious here—the *inside* of his shorts!"

Sydney wrinkled her nose. "*Eeeuw!* What did you do?"

"I told him it was on me." Francie rolled her eyes. "Anyway, after that I told Terwilliger I had a migraine and got off early." She pushed a tall glass of soda toward Sydney. "Here, I took the liberty of getting you a drink."

"Thanks," Sydney said, slipping out of her dove gray cardigan and hanging it on the back of her chair.

Francie took a long sip from her own glass and settled back in her seat. "So," she began brightly. "How was *your* day?"

"It was great," Sydney confessed with a smile. "Look at this." She reached into her purse and pulled out the pager, running her hand over its smooth, shiny surface. "My boss gave it to me today. Said I should wear it all the time."

"Let me see." Sydney handed the beeper to

Francie. "How cool! So . . . does this mean they're, like, giving you more responsibility now? Like maybe they're going to be promoting you soon?"

Sydney shrugged slightly, but her smile widened. "I think so."

"Wait a minute." Francie scowled. "Does this mean they can call you *anytime*? Like during class? Or when we're hanging out like this?"

Sydney thought for a moment. "I don't know. Maybe. I'm not exactly *that* important to them. At least not yet."

Francie tilted her head, studying her closely. "You know something? I think this job has been really good for you. You've really changed since you started there. You seem more, I don't know, together. More confident."

Sydney smoothed the puckers from her dress lining. *She's right,* she told herself. Ever since she had started working for the CIA, she'd felt more powerful. Not just because she could kickbox and shoot guns now. But because for the first time in her life, she had a purpose. A noble purpose.

"I know you had your doubts when you started," Francie went on. She leaned across the table, her eyes glimmering from the light of the candle sconce. "I guess banking probably isn't the most exciting work around. But you know, it takes all kinds of people in the world. And if banking is your thing, then I say more power to you!"

Francie handed back the pager. Sydney held it loosely in her palm, staring down at her face reflected in the smudged tabletop. She might not have been sure in the beginning, but she knew now that working for the agency was definitely for her. She'd excelled at things before—her classes, running track, theater arts. But this was the first time it truly mattered to her. And since her dad never seemed to care about her accomplishments, this was also the first time it mattered to someone else. The people at the agency thought she was strong, capable, and reliable. They trusted her with their secrets (some of them, anyway), and now they were entrusting her with a twenty-four-seven pager. All her hard work seemed to be paying off.

"See? That's what I'm talking about," Francie exclaimed, wagging a finger at her.

"What?" Sydney asked.

"You're smiling! I've been around you twenty-four-seven since last summer and I've never seen you smile this much. You're practically glowing. Everyone notices. Guys especially. See that one at the bar? The one in the leather bomber? He's totally been checking you out."

Sydney glanced toward the bar, but all she could see was the back of the guy's head and black leather jacket. She looked back at Francie and rolled her eyes. "He's probably staring at *you*."

"Uh-uh." Francie shook her head. "Believe me, I would have noticed if he was. Since Baxter and I broke up, I've been looking for some sort of worthy replacement. I scoped out all the guys the first five minutes I was here. Nothing."

"I still don't understand why you dumped Baxter," Sydney said, stirring her straw in her glass.

Francie made a face. "Because! All he wanted to do was make out. I don't know about you, but for me there's got to be more to a relationship than just the physical stuff." All at once, she sat up straight and stared past Sydney toward the front door. "Oh, my god! A major hottie just walked in. He looks just like Antonio Banderas!"

Sydney started to turn around.

"No! Don't look!" Francie whispered. "I don't want it to seem obvious."

"If you think he's so cute, why don't you try to catch his eye?" Sydney asked, laughing.

Francie looked thoughtful for a moment. "I will if you will," she said with a sly grin. "The guy at the bar is kind of hunky. Maybe *you* should check *him* out."

"Come on, Fran," Sydney began, shaking her head. "You know I don't want—"

"Hey, all I'm saying is look at him. Just see if he's your type. That's all."

Sydney sat back in her chair and casually let her gaze wander in that direction. The guy was leaning against the bar. From what she could see, he was okay-looking. Tall, with long wavy brown hair. Maybe a goatee. She couldn't be sure since the rest of his profile was partially hidden behind the collar of his jacket.

A dense heaviness suddenly pressed down on her. Something wasn't right. The club was warm and sultry. Stifling. All sweaty patrons and heavy cigarette smoke. So why was the guy still wearing a thick leather coat? She let her eyes pass over him again. Sure enough, his left arm was bent awkwardly at his side. Instead of resting on the edge of the counter, it was pressed against his jacket as if holding it shut.

Just then, the guy turned toward her. He appeared to be surveying the collection of signed celebrity photographs on the wall when his eyes suddenly locked onto hers. She stared back at him and he quickly glanced away, but not before she had gotten a clear view of his face.

She'd seen him before—she was sure of it. Yesterday afternoon when she was eating lunch on campus with Francie, he'd been sitting at a nearby table in sunglasses and a baseball cap. He was following her. But why? And who sent him? Wilson wouldn't still be sending people to spy on her. Or would he?

"So what do you think?" Francie whispered after the man turned back around. "Don't lie, Syd. I can tell you're interested. He is cute, don't you think?"

"Uh, yeah. He's intriguing all right," Sydney replied.

"Maybe you could go over and introduce yourself?" Francie sucked in her breath. "Oh, my god. Antonio's twin just sat down at the table behind you. I'm going to go freshen up. Will you watch my drink?"

"Sure," Sydney replied absently as Francie stood and walked off toward the restrooms. "No problem." Her mind was tilting and spinning like a carnival ride. Thoughts and emotions whirled past, but she couldn't hold on to any one of them.

It just didn't make sense. Why would someone be following her?

"Only one way to find out," she mumbled

under her breath. "Time for a refill." She scooped up Francie's half-full glass of soda and sauntered over to the bar, plastering a demure smile onto her face in case Francie should return and see her.

As she approached, the guy seemed to catch sight of her. He didn't look up, instead hunching his shoulders and pressing his elbows closer to his body.

"Hi, I'm Sydney," she said brightly, sliding onto the stool beside him.

The guy gave her a quick nod and glanced in the opposite direction.

Sydney leaned closer, tilting her head like the flirty girl in the body language manual. "Why are you following me?" she muttered through her smile.

"I don't know what you're talking about," he replied brusquely.

"You ought to be more careful. I saw you on campus today, and now here you are in the same bar as me with a gun in your coat," she murmured, still grinning and twisting a lock of hair around her index finger. "Now, do you want to tell me what's going on? Or should I make a scene and tell the bouncer you're bothering me?"

He looked right at her and smirked. "*You* ought to be more careful," he muttered. "They don't like it when one of us gets too big for our britches." He took one final swallow of his drink, stood, and casually strode out of the club.

They? Us? So the agency was following her! But why? And why would they be giving her a pager and heaping her with praise if they still weren't sure about her? Her pride, which had been soaring only a few moments before, now came crashing down to earth.

She was just sitting back down in her chair when Francie emerged from the bathroom. She took one look at Sydney, glanced over at the bar, and frowned.

"Did you go talk to him?" she asked, returning to her seat.

"Yep," Sydney said.

"So?" Francie asked almost hesitantly, as if she already knew the answer. "How did it go?"

"He was . . . involved," Sydney replied, trying to look sufficiently resigned. It wasn't too hard. They really must not trust her very much if she was still being tailed after eight months on the job. "Involved with someone else."

"What?" Francie cried. "He already had a girlfriend and he was making eyes at you! What a jerk!"

"I know," Sydney said, her voice indignant and dejected all at once. She lifted her pager, stared at it a moment, and then tossed it unceremoniously into her open purse. "I guess it just goes to show you have to be really careful who you trust."

*   *   *

Sydney stalked into Wilson's office and slammed the door behind her so hard it rattled the framed Years of Service awards that hung on the wall. "You sent him, didn't you?" she said hotly.

Wilson glanced up, looking only mildly surprised—as if he'd expected her to come barging in at nine-thirty instead of nine-fifteen. "Good morning to you too, Sydney," he said calmly.

"Why?" she asked, marching up to his desk. "Why am I being followed?"

Zero emotion. "Why don't you sit down?" he asked, gesturing toward her desk.

Sydney ignored him. "I don't understand," she tried again, in a hard, measured tone. "I've been working my butt off for eight months and you guys still don't believe in me? Why did you give me that pager and lead me to believe I was important— and then send the lamest"—she made air quotes— "'covert agent' to spy on me?"

"Sydney, I—"

"I mean, okay. So maybe you're afraid you made a mistake with me," she went on, hands on her hips. "Maybe you guys aren't happy with the way I'm turning out. But why can't you just talk to me about it?"

"Sydney!" Wilson shouted, rising from his chair.

She blinked, her mouth still open.

"Take your seat. Now."

Still pouting, Sydney trudged over to her usual chair and slumped into it.

"We *are* happy with the way you're turning out, Sydney," Wilson said, settling back into his seat. "In fact, we've never had a trainee move up as rapidly as you have."

"Really?" Sydney asked in a doubtful whisper. This was not what she'd expected at all. She'd come in ready to do battle and instead he was showering her with more praise? She narrowed her eyes and studied him, checking for signs of a trap.

"Look at this," Wilson said, reaching into a drawer and pulling out a thick black file. "All of your intelligence tests come back with record-setting results. Weapons, combat skills, linguistics, understanding of operations—you're learning them all at a phenomenal rate. You've set records in practically every area. Even your periodic physicals come back flawless. Face it, Sydney. You're the perfect recruit."

"I am?" She ran her finger along the file's edge, shifting her weight in her chair. The raging scorn she'd been fueling herself with was suddenly gone. Now she just felt small and shy. Even though she loved hearing what Wilson had to say, it also made her uneasy. She'd never been taught how to handle a compliment. And the fact that it came from Wilson, who was so like her father and yet so different, made it even harder to know what to do.

A sudden thought made her sit up straight. "But the man following me. You still haven't told me why you did that," she added, a slight edge creeping back into her voice. She wasn't going to let some nice words derail her from her original purpose.

"It's standard procedure with all new recruits, Sydney—the only difference being that others rarely pick up on it," Wilson replied. He paused. "In our line of work, we have to take the utmost precautions with security. I hope you can appreciate that. It's for your well-being as well as ours."

"Oh," Sydney said, wilting slightly. "So . . . this is only until my training is over?"

Wilson nodded. "Although you will always be under surveillance to some degree. Never forget that."

Sydney sighed defeatedly, her eyes round and sorrowful. "Listen, I'm sorry. When I saw that guy, I just thought . . . well, I guess I just assumed . . ."

Wilson lifted his hand, silencing her. "It's all right. Perfectly understandable. But in the future, should you ID your tails, do *not* approach them. It could expose you both and endanger the whole agency."

"Right. Sorry," she repeated, staring down at her lap.

She heard the squeak of Wilson's chair as he leaned back in it. "You know," he began in a slightly amused tone, "that's probably your only weakness."

Sydney glanced back up at him. "What's that?"

"Your temper," he replied, looking her right in the eyes. "You need to learn how to divorce your emotions from your work. Strong feelings can only get an agent in trouble."

She frowned slightly, wondering exactly what he meant. But before she could say anything, Wilson sat forward and placed his hands on his desk.

"That said, I want you to know that your superiors at headquarters are quite pleased with your progress." He reached into another lower drawer and pulled out a large manila envelope. "You've been working very hard, Sydney. And we wanted to give you this as a token of our appreciation. I was going to page you to come in so I could surprise you, but since you're already here . . ."

A small current of warmth coursed through her as she watched him hold out the envelope, his lips tucked against his teeth in an awkward grin. She'd never seen Wilson look ill at ease before. And he was actually giving her a present. A reward of sorts. This was even better than the pager.

"Thanks," she said, reaching for the packet. Whatever it was, it was extremely light. Slowly and carefully, she pulled back the top flap and turned the envelope upside down until a small rectangular card slid out. She quickly scanned the tiny writing and gasped. "A ticket to Raul Sandoval? For tonight's show?"

Wilson nodded, looking immensely pleased. "A front-row seat. We remembered you mentioning that you liked his music and got it for you."

Talk about attention to detail! "But . . . but the show's been sold out for weeks! How did you wrangle it?"

"Let's just say we have our connections," he replied with an actual wink.

"Thank you so much!" she exclaimed, shaking her head in astonishment. "I . . . I don't know what to say." She was about to leave when Wilson cleared his throat.

"Sydney?" Wilson said, ducking his head slightly. "Before you're off, I have a small favor."

"What's that?"

"I don't know if you know this or not, but I have a daughter," he said, allowing a small smile to make its way across his face. "Her name is Claire. She's eleven."

Sydney grinned back, amazed at this newer, gentler side of her boss. "No. I didn't know," she said, pleased to be confided in.

"Yes. Well, she's a big fan of Raul Sandoval, but I've told her she's much too young to go to a concert."

"Right. Of course," Sydney agreed.

"So I was wondering, would you mind trying to take some photos of the show? Claire's birthday is coming up at the end of May and it would mean the world to her."

Sydney nodded. "Sure. No problem. But . . . aren't cameras forbidden inside the arena?"

"Yes. I thought of something, though." He

reached into the pocket of his dark blue blazer and pulled out a large silver arm cuff, which he held out to her, an awkward expression on his face. "Would you mind wearing this?"

"Um . . . okay," she said, picking up the cuff and holding it up to the light. "So is this some valuable secret-society bracelet that will allow me to bring in a camera?"

"Sort of. It's a valuable secret-society bracelet that *is* a camera. I'm 'borrowing' it from our operations-technology supply," he explained with a wry smile. "See this large black stone? That's the lens. Aim it at whatever you want a picture of and press this smaller, red stone on the side."

"What about this green one?" she asked, pointing to the other stone in the design.

"That's nothing. Just for aesthetics."

"Oh." She pushed up the sleeve of her shirt and placed the bangle on her arm, the metal hard and cool against her skin.

"Don't wear it around here," Wilson said somewhat nervously, nodding in the direction of the corridor. "They won't miss it from the lab, but agents aren't supposed to mix work with their personal life." He lowered his voice. "I could get into real trouble."

"I won't breathe a word." Sydney was just

about to slip the bracelet into her purse when Wilson touched her elbow. 153 — RECRUITED

"Listen," he said apologetically. "If you're at all uncomfortable about doing this for me, you really don't have to."

Sydney smiled back. "Are you kidding? It's my pleasure. I remember what it feels like to be eleven and in love with the pop star du jour. I'm happy to help you out." Wilson wasn't a hardened CIA operative but a caring father. She couldn't help feeling a tug of longing. If only her own father had been more this way . . .

But he wasn't. Her dad was never going to change, and she should just accept that. In the meantime, if Wilson was asking her to do a little rule bending for the sake of his daughter, then she was going to do everything in her power to help him out.

"Thanks, Sydney."

"Guess I better go." She shouldered her purse and turned toward the door.

"Wait," Wilson called. "One more thing. Something important."

Sydney wheeled back around.

"I need to take you to headquarters. Sloane wants to meet you."

* * *

Sydney was barely aware of her feet moving as she followed Wilson into the Credit Dauphine lobby.

She didn't know who Sloane was. She didn't know *where* he was. She didn't know *why* he wanted to see her, *what* he would do when he saw her, or *how* she was even going to get there. All she knew was when it would be. This morning—*now*. If only she'd had more time to prepare. Maybe then she wouldn't feel so shaky.

Wilson didn't say a word as they crossed the lobby's polished marble floor and stepped into an open elevator. Sydney discreetly smoothed the front of her pants and pushed a few stray strands of hair off her face.

The elevator door shut and Wilson flipped open a small box at the bottom of the button panel. Then he inserted a small metal key and turned it in a three-quarters circle clockwise. Sydney felt a slight jolt and the elevator began going down.

She waited for the car to stop on one of the subterranean parking levels. But it didn't. Instead the elevator kept descending, past all the basement and parking floors, until the lighted number display showed nothing but a horizontal line. Sydney stood ramrod straight, trying to fend off a serious case of nerves. Judging by the length of the ride, they must be more than five stories underground. Where, exactly, did Wilson park his car? The Bat Cave?

Eventually the elevator settled to a stop and the doors slid open. Sydney and Wilson stepped into a small, bare, square-paneled room. She wondered if it might be another elevator, but the floor felt too solid beneath her feet. Her eyes had just finished adjusting to the harsh overhead lights and brilliant white of the walls when an intense red beam suddenly illuminated the room. She blinked as the ray traveled over her and Wilson and then quickly went out.

What was that? she wondered. *Some sort of scan?* She wanted to ask Wilson, but he seemed so deep into work mode, she decided against it.

Just then, the wall in front of them parted, revealing a vast office space. "This is headquarters," Wilson said as they stepped out of the white room. "We're now six stories beneath the bank building. Only personnel with the highest security clearance have access to this area. You are now one of them."

Sydney acknowledged this with a brief nod. *I'm in,* she thought. A fierce pride overcame her, freezing her grin into place.

They stepped out of the white room and made

their way forward. The work area was a labyrinth of glass partitions and stone pillars wrapped in thick wires and cables. Men and women of different ages and ethnicities rushed to and fro, many of them nodding to Wilson, some stopping to mutter a few words in his ear. No one gave Sydney a passing glance. She was amazed at how normal the men and women looked. If she had passed them on the street in their neutral-colored business suits, she would have assumed they were run-of-the mill bankers, marketers, or sales reps. But they weren't. They were spies. Real-life, undercover CIA *spies*. She knew it was true, and yet her brain still couldn't quite grasp it. What looked like a typical office staff Sydney saw as gallant heroes, working together to stop the terrors of the world. And *she* was one of them!

Sydney hurriedly tried to walk alongside Wilson, but his broad shoulders caused her to veer into the oncoming pedestrian traffic and she ended up bumping shoulders with a tall, dignified-looking black man.

"I'm so sorry," she apologized.

"It's all right," he said, flashing her a wide, warm smile. "I wasn't looking where I was going."

The man resumed his pace down the corridor and Sydney quickly caught up to Wilson. A few seconds later, they came to a short row of offices and stopped in front of one of the doors.

"Here we are," Wilson announced. He lifted his brows and stared at her questioningly. She smiled and nodded. He raised his fist and knocked a couple of times. Eventually they heard a muffled "Come in."

Wilson opened the door and gestured for her to enter. Sydney straightened her back, took a deep breath, and walked in.

The man she was there to see was standing just inside the room. He had dark, thinning hair and a short, grizzled beard. "So you're Sydney Bristow," he said, smiling faintly.

"Yes, sir." She guessed he was around fifty.

"I'm Arvin Sloane. Welcome to SD-6."

"Thanks," she replied, shaking his hand. Then she glanced over at Wilson. "What's SD-6?"

Wilson shut the door and motioned for her to take a seat. She and Wilson sat down on padded chairs facing a wide wooden desk, while Sloane took his place in the high-backed leather chair behind it.

"There are a few things you need to know now that you are at this level of your transition," Wilson said, his face a mask of seriousness. "SD-6 is a code term for us. What we are, what you are now a part of, is a black ops division of the CIA."

Sydney furrowed her brow. "Black ops?" she repeated.

"What that means," Sloane said, leaning forward, "is that our unit is highly classified, even within the agency itself. Only a few top-ranking officials in government know about us."

"I don't understand," she said, shaking her head. "Why are you a secret to your own country?"

"Because the fewer people who know our identities, the better we're able to do our job." He paused briefly, his hand sweeping toward the office window and the bustle outside. "All these people you see here, they are an elite force of agents whose main objective is to seek out and stop anything that threatens national security—even if it seems to run counter to other government policy. We risk our lives when other people can't even risk their images."

"I see," she said, even though she still couldn't quite fathom what he was saying. So not only was she part of an undercover agency, her section was even undercover *within* the undercover agency. Or something like that.

"You'll be finding out more as you move up," Sloane went on, seeming to sense her confusion. "Which, I must add, should be very soon. I've been hearing a lot about you, Miss Bristow. We're all very pleased with your progress."

"Thank you, sir," she replied. Her pride seemed to ignite and a warm feeling coursed through her. She looked over and smiled at Wilson, who gave her an encouraging nod. "I'm very honored to be a part of this, sir."

Sloane's gaze intensified. For a moment he appeared to be studying her, as if she were an interesting lab specimen. But just as Sydney was beginning to feel uncomfortable, his face broke into a grin. "Well," he said as he stood up, signaling the end of the conversation, "very soon now you will be ready to go out on field missions, and I just wanted to get a sense of who you are."

"Yes, sir," she responded. "Thank you very much." She and Wilson rose from their seats.

"Thank you for coming by, Miss Bristow. I'm sure we'll talk again soon," Sloane said, lightly clasping her hand. "Oh, and Miss Bristow? Enjoy the concert."

10

SYDNEY STOOD IN FRONT of the full-length mirror Francie had mounted on her closet door and stared at her reflection. The transformation was amazing. She almost looked like a different person.

Staring back at her was a tall, tough girl in black leather pants and matching leather vest. The top layer of her hair was teased into stiff spikes that stood up on her head at a thirty-degree angle. Her eyes were ringed with thick dark lines, and a deep, bloodlike red covered her full lips. On her right ear, an inch-long spike hung from a metal cuff. And a large silver armband shone on her left forearm.

She had decided to dress the part of a rock groupie. It began when she realized the silver arm cuff Wilson had given her didn't go with anything she'd typically wear. The last thing she wanted was for it to stand out and make people suspicious. So she decided to design an outfit around it.

She raised her fist into the air and assumed the cocky semi-snarl of a rocker. "Yeah," she said to her image. "Sydney Vicious!"

This was going to be fun. She hadn't worn the outfit since she and Francie dressed as biker chicks for Halloween. Sydney laughed, remembering the look on their R.A.'s face when they walked out of the dorm, Francie holding a whip and barely able to walk in her tight vinyl skirt and thigh-high boots.

As a little kid, Sydney had loved dressing up and pretending to be other people. A fairy princess. A black cat. A swashbuckling pirate. Costumes gave her confidence. They let her play mental tricks on herself, getting her to do things she'd never be able to do when she was plain old Sydney.

Her theatrical skills and knack for dialects

brought all sorts of other perks too. Whenever she and her boarding school friends had wanted to go clothes shopping, they would put on their most fashionable dresses and pretend to be rich, snooty English tourists. The saleswomen at the posh boutiques would practically mow each other down to assist them. Of course, had they known who the girls really were, they probably wouldn't have even wasted breath insulting them.

Sydney sighed. She wanted to keep in touch with her old friends, but it was hard enough keeping in touch with her new ones.

If only Francie could go with her tonight. Francie loved Raul Sandoval even more than Sydney. In fact, she was the one who had converted Sydney to his music. But there was only one ticket, and it would have appeared totally ungrateful to have asked Wilson for another. Plus, she'd have to explain why she was fiddling with a strange arm cuff all night—and how she'd managed to score front-row tickets to a sold-out show in the first place.

All of a sudden, Sydney heard a key scratch in the front-door lock. Panic surged through her and she instinctively searched for a place to hide. But it was too late. Francie burst into the room, wearing her waitressing uniform and a scowl. She took two weary steps toward her bed, then paused and stared openmouthed at Sydney.

"Uh . . . hello? Who are you and what have you done with my roommate?"

"Hey, Francie," Sydney said with a sheepish grin. "I . . . I thought you were at work tonight."

"I was. Terwilliger's heart must have grown ten times today. He let us off early since the place was totally dead. Probably because everyone's going to Raul Sandoval's show. Lucky bastards." She threw her bag onto her bed while continuing to gape at Sydney. "Okay, now. Out with it. Why are you dressed like that?"

Sydney's mind reeled. "I'm . . . going to a theme party," she blurted out.

"Really?" Francie's eyes sparkled. "How fun! Can I come?"

"Um, I don't know. The thing is . . ." She paused, suddenly sweltering in her leather ensemble. "I'm sort of going to see a guy."

"Get out!" Francie exclaimed, her smile as wide as her eyes. "You have a date! And you didn't tell me!"

Sydney held up a hand. "No, no! It's not a date. I'm sort of just . . . checking him out. You know? But I would like to go by myself. In case something happens."

Francie's mouth curled into a sly grin. "Say no more. I totally understand."

"Really?" Sydney asked guiltily. "You sure you're not mad?"

"Of course not." Francie sat on the edge of her bed and began pulling off her shoes. "Besides, I've got big plans myself. I'm going to take a long hot bath and then watch TNT. They're showing *Philadelphia Story* tonight. You know what a sucker I am for Cary Grant."

"Right," Sydney said, breathing a sigh of relief. That had been close. "Well, have a good time." She grabbed her car keys off her dresser and headed for the door. "Bye."

"Hey, wait!" Francie cried. "Don't you want to borrow my whip?"

Sydney laughed. "Um, no. I don't think so."

"Suit yourself," Francie called out as Sydney stepped into the hall. "Maybe on the next date, then?"

*   *   *

By the time Sydney arrived at the Las Cruces Arena, the place was spilling over with people. She joined the throngs of concertgoers heading for the doors and noticed several other fans wearing similar leather ensembles.

She was glad she'd dressed up. She would have

felt funny otherwise, going to a concert on her own. Her getup helped her feel like a tough, wild rebel. She even walked differently, her black engineer boots taking long, swaggering strides as she strutted up to the front entrance.

Sydney flashed her ticket to the guy at the front turnstile.

"Whoa. First row," he exclaimed, pushing up his glasses as he surveyed the ticket. "Okay. Take the escalator down to the basement level and an usher will show you to your seat. Oh, and security wants us to remind people not to start a mosh pit."

"Yeah, whatever," Sydney said, snatching back her ticket and loping toward a nearby escalator.

She felt incredibly brash and sassy. As she strode down the length of the concourse, she could feel people staring at her. Groups of girls shot her snooty up-and-down glances, while guys tended to focus on the large zipper of her tight leather vest. Sydney sauntered along, pretending to be oblivious, all the while enjoying the attention.

Throughout the arena, gigantic photos of Raul Sandoval's face hung from the ceiling. Everywhere she looked she could see his frothy black curls, sultry eyes, and seductive grin. The guy was definitely sexy. And even though he seemed a little too stormy and self-aware to be her type, she could see how Francie and Claire Wilson could drool over him.

A stammering high-school-aged guy led her down to her seat. Sydney was amazed at how fantastic it was. The stage was directly in front of her, right at neck level. At the moment all she could see were thick burgundy drapes and two towering stacks of speakers flanking either side. Below them, two truck-sized men stood glaring at the assembling crowd.

"Ra-ul! Ra-ul! Ra-ul!" the onlookers began to shout.

And then it began. The lights came down. The curtains opened. And high-pitched screeches of electric guitars blared from the walls of speakers.

A spotlight shone down from the ceiling, illuminating a tall figure. He stood in front of a microphone in the center of the stage, wearing a ripped white T-shirt and brown leather pants. A starburst Les Paul guitar was slung across his chest. Raul Sandoval.

He raised his arms in a messiah-like gesture and the crowd went wild. "Hello, Los Angeles!" he cried. Then with a nod toward his band, he bent over his guitar and began to play.

Sydney had never seen such a concert in her

life. The music was almost excruciatingly loud. The entire arena quaked, and she could feel the throbbing of the bass guitar in the center of her rib cage. But it was thrilling, too. Sydney closed her eyes and let herself merge with the energy, dancing along to all of the songs. Occasionally she would stop, fiddle with her armband, and snap a few shots.

There was plenty to photograph. Sandoval strutted up and down the stage to a barrage of flashbulbs and fireworks. Exotic dancers rose up through trapdoors. In keeping with his rebellious lyrics, Sandoval's face became a fixed snarl, and he thrashed and whaled on his guitar as if he were furious with it.

Forty minutes into the show, the music suddenly died down to the volume of a distant storm. Sandoval grabbed a microphone and walked to the edge of the stage, looming right above Sydney. All the lights went out except for a single white spot beaming down on him. He stood there panting, beads of sweat glistening on his body like rhinestones. Girlish squeals erupted from every part of the arena. Sandoval gazed out at the audience, and then his eyes fell on Sydney. He smiled. Sydney froze in surprise. Then the music swelled and Sandoval began to sing in Spanish.

It was a love ballad. She mentally translated

the lyrics as she watched him crooning into the mike, eyes closed, his left hand moving up and down with the melody.

You've caged my heart.
Your eyes, your lips, your laugh,
   your touch are the walls of my prison.
I cannot escape, and yet
I do not want to.
I live at your command.
I love at your command.
I die at your command.

All around her, couples stood with their arms entwined, swaying. Sydney felt a pang. For the first time that night she was aware of being alone. She found herself thinking of the nameless young agent, and how it might feel to lean up against him, enfolded in his long, muscular arms.

Get over it, she told herself. *Like that would ever happen anyway. Just forget about the guy and have fun.*

As Sandoval crooned and emoted, Sydney twisted her bracelet so that the center stone pointed right at him. Then she pressed the red stone to the side. *Click.*

There, she thought smugly. Claire would have that one under her pillow for sure.

After a long, wailing final note, the song ended and the rest of the stage lights came up. Sydney cheered along with the rest of the crowd, some of whom were throwing items of clothing onto the stage. Sandoval picked up a blue scarf and mopped his face with it. Then he raised his arms and waved to the audience. Women everywhere screamed. Sydney ended up getting slammed hard against the stage as two girls behind her pushed forward toward Sandoval.

"Give it to me! To me!" they screamed.

Sandoval kneeled down directly in front of Sydney. He looked right at her, a brash, seductive smile slowly making its way across his face. Then he reached out and handed her the blue scarf.

Sydney stood there blinking for a moment, still gasping from the sudden impact with the stage. Eventually she lifted her hand and snatched the sweaty rag with her fingertips. "Thanks," she murmured, blushing in spite of herself. Sandoval might be a total poser, but he was kind of cute.

The band started up again. Sandoval gave Sydney one last look and paraded back upstage. All around her, girls were giving Sydney death glares.

She quickly shoved the scarf into her bra and went back into her tough girl stance. She really hoped she wouldn't have to use her combat skills on any crazed fans.

For the rest of the show Sandoval stuck with his usual loud, raucous rock songs. Sydney danced and whooped and took several more excellent shots for Claire. After a big, cheesy final number, complete with a light show, pyrotechnics, and lots and lots of piped-in smoke, Sandoval wrapped up his set, thanked the audience, and walked backstage.

"Ra-ul! Ra-ul! Ra-ul!" the crowd began chanting.

"Hey, you!" Sydney glanced to her left and saw one of the bodybuilder-type bouncers walking over, pointing right at her.

Her stomach tightened. Maybe he'd seen her toying with the bracelet and figured out it was a camera. What if they confiscated it? She could get Wilson into major trouble, as well as herself. Maybe even endanger the whole agency!

"Come with me," the man said gruffly.

"Why?" she asked, trying to act casual.

He looked surprised. "Don't you want to go backstage?"

Sydney relaxed. Sandoval had taken a liking

to her. Visions of sleazy spandex-clad girls at Kiss reunion concerts flashed through her mind. She was about to say no. But then Claire popped into her mind. *I'll get his autograph,* she thought excitedly. Claire would totally rule at her middle school with that. And Wilson wouldn't believe it!

"Yeah," she replied. "Of course."

The man hooked his hand around Sydney's upper arm and led her down the aisle. Sydney didn't appreciate being yanked along like a preschooler, but after seeing how freaked out some of the fans could get, she didn't mind the precaution. They walked to the side of the stage, past the wall of speakers, up a few steps, and behind some black curtains. Then they meandered through the stacks of equipment cases until they reached a wooden door. The man raised his fist and knocked three times.

Another surly-looking muscleman opened the door, took one glance at them, and ushered them inside. Sydney found herself inside a long, white-walled dressing room. At the far end was a wide vanity topped with a length of mirror ringed with lightbulbs. On the right side of the room stood a cloth-draped table covered with sandwiches and chunks of cantaloupe and pineapple. And to the left several black-clad people sat talking on a pair of sofas, a cloud of cigarette smoke hovering above them.

In the middle of the room stood Sandoval himself, shoving his arms into the sleeves of a red silk shirt.

Sydney grinned. She couldn't believe she was backstage with Raul Sandoval! If only she could share this with Francie!

Sandoval turned around and spotted Sydney. "Ah, *la señorita,*" he said. "Hello. I am Raul. How are you?" He held out his hand.

"Fine. Thanks." She grasped his palm and was about to give it a shake when he suddenly lifted her hand to his lips and kissed it. In the mirror behind him, she could see her cheeks flame to match her lipstick.

"Jou enjoy the show?" he asked in his thick Cuban accent. He released her hand and started to button his shirt, stopping halfway up.

"Yeah," she replied, trying hard to regain the cool, sassy edge in her voice. "Hey, could I get your autograph?"

"Of course." He reached for the pad of paper and pen lying next to the phone on the end table. "And jou are?"

"Could you make it out to Claire?"

"Claire. Jes. Ees a lovely name." He smiled at her and then hastily scribbled, *To Claire—All my love, Raul S.* Then he ripped off the sheet and handed it to her.

"Thanks," she said, slipping it into her back pocket. *All righty. Vámonos!*

In the distance, the sounds of the crowd stomping and chanting his name grew louder.

"*Oye. La gente me está llamando,*" he said, nodding in the direction of the stage. "My fans are calling. I must go."

"Oh. Right," she agreed. "I guess I better take off too."

Sandoval burst out laughing. "No, I don't think so," he said, placing his hand on her shoulder and gently pushing her toward one of the couches. "You will stay here with my friends. I will do my encores and come back."

"Um . . . okay," she said, landing on the end of an overstuffed chenille sofa.

"*Ahora, vámanos,*" Sandoval said to his band, and they walked out of the room. The roar of the crowd grew louder as the door swung open, then muffled once again as it shut behind them.

Sydney glanced around at the rest of Sandoval's entourage. There were three Goth girls in tight black dresses and raccoon-like eye makeup, a couple of guys in dark suits and sunglasses, and another muscle-bound bouncer standing near the door—this one a big bald Mr. Clean clone. *So Sandoval wants me to hang out with his crowd?* she wondered. She obviously looked as if she belonged, but she certainly didn't feel it.

One of the Goth girls with long straight black hair stared at her from the opposite couch. Sydney nodded in greeting, but the girl simply blew cigarette smoke at her and turned away.

Charming, she thought. Oh, well. She might as well get some backstage shots while she was there. Then when Sandoval got back, she could thank him and leave.

While the others smoked and chatted about the show in bored-sounding tones, Sydney slouched back against the sofa cushions and pretended to play with her armband.

That's when she noticed it. Looking down at the bracelet, she saw that one of the stones was missing. Her panic faded a bit when she realized it was only the green stone—not the one hiding the lens or its trigger. Still, she felt bad. Wilson had entrusted her with this and now it was damaged. Most likely it had popped off when those demented fans shoved her into the stage. It was probably too late to try to find the missing piece and mend it herself.

She only hoped Wilson's disappointment might be lessened by the autograph and photos. To be extra sure, she added shots of Sandoval's guitar case, his gloomy-looking groupies, and even Mr. Clean. She figured Claire might enjoy getting the full story. Plus, she really didn't have anything else to do.

After a couple minutes, Mr. Clean opened the door and said in a gravelly voice, "All right. Time to move on to the hotel and get the party started."

"What about Raul?" asked the smoke-blowing Goth girl.

"He's got some business. He'll join us later."

"Fine," said the girl irritably. She and the rest of the entourage pushed themselves off the sofas and ambled out the door.

Sydney stayed in her seat, wondering what to do. After a moment, the bald bouncer came and stood in front of her, his arms folded across his chest impatiently.

"Me too?" Sydney asked.

He looked at her as if she were an imbecile. "He gave you the scarf didn't he?"

"Um, yeah. So?"

"*So*, it means he chose you." He gave her a

look that said he thought she was the world's biggest dope. "You get to hang out with him tonight."

"Oh, but . . . but I'm not . . ." She stood up and took a breath. "Sorry, but I don't think I can go with you guys."

At this, Mr. Clean stiffened and glared at her. "Mr. Sandoval is expecting you to wait for him," he growled, inching close enough for her to see the blood vessels in his eyes. "You got a problem with that?"

Sydney blinked at him. Her eyes took in his angry sneer, his baseball-sized arm muscles, and the unmistakable bulge of a handgun inside his leather blazer. Obviously Sandoval ran with a really rough crowd. If she said no, it might start a fight—a fight she would probably lose. Even if she didn't, she could end up being questioned by the cops, and what would SD-6 think of that? Especially with her wearing one of their government-issue op-tech devices without clearance?

"No. I don't have a problem," she replied, meeting his stare defiantly.

His posture relaxed slightly and his mouth curled into a malicious smile. "Good. Now why don't you do like I asked and go down to the limos waiting for us?"

Sydney could tell that even though he phrased his last comment as a question, he really wasn't giving her an option. "Fine. Whatever," she muttered as she stalked past him and strode out the door.

Okay, Syd. Think fast, she told herself. *There's got to be a way out of this.*

11

SYDNEY TROMPED AFTER SANDOVAL'S entourage as they made their way through the twisting, narrow passageways of the backstage area. The light was dim and Sydney could just make out the groupie girl's skull-shaped metal hair clip bouncing in front of her. Behind her, Mr. Clean's ragged breathing reminded her of his menacing presence.

She had to find a way out of this. Not only did these people make her nervous, she was also extremely tense about the bracelet. If she went with these guys, it could accidentally fall into their hands. And what if they discovered what it could do? Besides, she didn't want to risk any more damage to it, or to the photos inside.

But how would she ever convince Sandoval's goon to let her leave?

"Yuck. This place is the pits. That hall in San Francisco was so much nicer," whined one of the groupies near the front.

Sydney could hear a banging noise, and then another voice called, "Roland, this door is locked and there's stuff dripping from the ceiling! Are you sure this is the right way?"

Mr. Clean, aka Roland, grunted loudly and began pushing his way to the front of the pack. "Hang on. I've got the key," he grumbled.

As the others pressed forward, Sydney hung back. This was her chance. She quickly glanced around for a place to hide and noticed another corridor off to her left. As quietly as possible, she darted through the shadowy threshold and tiptoed away.

Sydney found herself in a tunnel-like hallway. It was almost completely dark and seemed to be sloping downward. Luckily, light from the floors above was shining through seams in the ceiling, slightly illuminating the path. She carefully made her way down, wondering what the party crowd would do when they discovered she was gone. Would they try to find her? Sydney doubted any of them would miss her much. Except maybe Sandoval. She got the feeling a pampered rock star like him was used to getting anything, and anyone, he wanted.

For close to twenty minutes, Sydney groped her way through the near-darkness, trying to locate an exit, or at least someone who could lead her to one. It seemed strange that she hadn't run into anyone yet. Either she had strayed into some deep, unused area of the concert hall, or the entire arena staff had already gone home for the night. She considered turning and going back the way she'd come, but she didn't want to risk bumping into someone from Sandoval's pack. Besides, she probably couldn't trace her exact path anyway since the passageway had already forked a few times.

She was getting tired and hungry, and her feet ached inside her boots. Eventually, she perched on a crate and pulled them off.

"Much better," she said as she flexed her toes and slowly rotated her ankles. How people could act tough when their arches were caving in was a major mystery.

Just then, she heard a noise. Down the corridor in front of her came the sound of muffled voices. *Finally!* She grabbed her boots and followed the light up ahead. Something that resembled a large truck-loading bay was coming into view. The voices grew louder, and she realized one of the people talking had a thick Cuban accent. It was Sandoval.

Sydney hesitated. Here was an exit, but she couldn't exactly go prancing past Sandoval without an explanation. Maybe if she waited long enough, he would leave.

She carefully crept forward and peered around the corner of the corridor. Sandoval was standing in the middle of the bay. Next to him was a heavy-set man in a dull gray suit. The gentleman looked too old and well-dressed to be a fan or a security guard. As she watched, the man lifted his right hand and took a puff on a thick brown cigar. Something was jarred in the recesses of Sydney's memory. She'd seen this guy somewhere before.

The man turned, exposing his profile to the light. Sydney suddenly felt a chill run through her. She knew exactly who he was now. He was Josef Levski, one of the ringleaders of the *Mercado de Sangre*—the Bloody Black Market.

Sydney remembered reading several files about them. They were a group of former Cold War operatives from all over Europe and Cuba. During the chaos that ensued after the fall of the Iron Curtain, they had raided the military arsenals of former Soviet satellite nations and sold their spoils to the highest bidder. They dealt with anyone, selling arms and intelligence to rogue militant groups and terrorists. Lately their operations had grown to include hunting intelligence officers and bringing their severed heads to enemy agencies for a cash reward. These guys were hard-core. They were loyal to no country and no leader, and there was no negotiating with them.

But why is Sandoval talking with them? she wondered. Instinctively, she raised her wrist and snapped a picture of the two men. Maybe Wilson could help her sort it out later. *If* she ever got out of there.

A paralyzing numbness suddenly shot through her body. *This is no coincidence,* she told herself. *SD-6 sent me here on purpose. The ticket, the camera . . . it was all just a setup to get me here!*

"There you are!" came a voice from behind her. All of a sudden, Sydney found herself being yanked backward by her upper arm. She stumbled but managed to regain her balance. Twisting around, she saw Roland sneering down at her, the top of his bald head gleaming in the half-light.

Without thinking, Sydney jabbed him in the breastbone with her free elbow. An expression of surprise crossed his features—and hers. *I just freaking hit a guy the size of Schwarzenegger!* she thought wildly as his hand automatically released its grasp on her arm. Before he could do anything further, she whirled her right leg around and kicked him in the ribs. He was still stumbling backward when she turned and ran away, her bare feet slapping against the concrete floor.

She didn't feel fear. In fact, she didn't feel anything. She was simply reacting. *If I get out of this,* she thought as adrenaline pumped through her veins, *I'll have to tell Yoav what a good job he did training me.*

Behind her, Sydney could hear Roland let out a bellow of rage. She scrambled around a nearby corner only to find that it was a dead end. Meanwhile, Roland's heavy tread was coming closer and closer.

Sydney veered behind a stack of speakers and held still, trying desperately to quiet the sound of her breathing. She heard Roland's rapid footfall echo off the nearby walls, then stop altogether.

"You better come out!" he yelled angrily, calling

her every curse word in the book. "You can't hide for long!"

Sydney remained frozen, straining to catch each tiny sound. She could hear Roland's panting and the shuffling of his boots against the floor. Her heart was hammering, but she forced herself to stay still as a statue, concentrating on every noise. Eventually the steps grew nearer and Roland's heavy breathing seemed only inches away. . . .

Wham! In a flash of vicious fury, Sydney threw her weight against the stack of speakers, causing them to fall. A tremendous rumble echoed through the hall, followed by a cry of surprise. Then all was quiet.

Sydney dashed around the fallen stack. Roland's unconscious doughy form lay beneath the heap. For a moment, she stood there, paralyzed. *I totally did it,* she thought, a smile flickering over her face. Then she sprang to life, pouring everything she had into a race to the loading bay. But no sooner had she rounded the corner than something jumped out of the shadows. Sydney thrust out her arms in defense, but it was too late. A bare-knuckled fist collided with the side of her head, knocking her flat. Sydney caught a brief glimpse of Sandoval's dark, angry eyes swirling above her.

Then everything went dark.

*   *   *

"Mmmm. Close the blinds, Francie. I have a headache," Sydney mumbled. She must have eaten something that didn't agree with her. Her gut was clenched, her neck was stiff, and it hurt to look at the light. Plus, some idiot was working a jackhammer in the distance.

She opened her eyes wider and realized she wasn't in her dorm room at all. The jackhammer was pounding inside her head. And instead of Francie lying curled up in the next bed over, America's reigning pop idol, Raul Sandoval, was leering at her from a nearby sofa.

They were back in the dressing room. Only this time they were alone. Sydney was sitting hunched over in a high-backed wooden chair, her arms pulled back and secured behind her. Wincing slightly, she looked back and saw he had bound her wrists together tightly with guitar strings, the wires cutting into her skin.

"So I meet jou again, Claire," Sandoval muttered. He pressed his palms together as if in prayer and raised them to his mouth. Then he shook his head, making *tsk-tsk* noises with his tongue. "Jou should have gone to the party, *niña*. How come jou didn't go?"

"I got lost," she lied, gazing at him with a

wounded expression. She knew now that Sandoval was dangerous. Not only was he mixed up with bad people, he was one of them. Her only hope of getting away alive was to keep up the frightened-bystander act. "I'm sorry if I went into some restricted area or something," she continued, blinking back tears. "Please, just let me go."

Sandoval narrowed his eyes at her. "Why did jou attack my bodyguard?"

"I . . . I thought he was trying to attack me," she replied meekly. "I was just trying to protect myself."

"Jou are very good at protecting jourself." He rose up and walked over to her, grabbing her chin roughly. "Too good."

Sydney's gaze darted to his eyes and away again. She couldn't believe she had ever thought Sandoval was attractive. Now he just looked menacing. His mouth was twisted sadistically, blue veins jutted out from his forehead, and his stare was cold and hard.

She had to keep up the innocent act. If he even suspected she worked for SD-6, he'd kill her for sure. "I took a self-defense class," she whimpered.

He scowled at her and let go of her chin with a rough toss. "That's some class, I think," he said. "Jou must learn fast."

"I've been taking it for months," she explained hoarsely. "Please, you've got to believe me. I didn't mean to do anything wrong." She stared at him imploringly, making her lower lip tremble for effect. *Damn Wilson and his "Oh, could you get a picture for my Claire? It's her birthday, Sydney. Please?" And damn SD-6!* How could they actually send her after a vicious rock-star anarchist without even a word of warning? All for a few lousy photos?

A sudden thought occurred to her. The bracelet! What if Sandoval found it? It could tip him off that she was a spy. Slowly and steadily, so as not to jerk her upper body, she stretched out the fingers of her right hand along her opposite wrist until they hit the cool, hard metal of the arm cuff. Thank god it was still there! She slid her index finger along the silver band and found that the two remaining stones were intact.

Suddenly she felt the guitar strings give slightly. A trill of optimism buzzed through her body, easing her headache and filling her with new strength. As subtly as possible, she began twisting her wrists back and forth, rejoicing as the tension gradually fell slack.

Sandoval continued to stare at her scornfully.

"Jou see, Claire. I have a problem," he said gravely. He pulled up a chair and sat down facing her. "Jou could be telling the truth, but I don't know for sure. But . . . I have a way to tell, I think." He reached down into his boot and pulled out a long, shiny dagger with a hilt of ornately carved ivory.

"Is beautiful, no?" he asked, waving the knife in front of her face. "I got it in the Sudan while I do business there. I had it made *especial*."

Sydney's eyes grew wide as the razor-sharp tip circled her nose, cheeks, and chin. *The man's a psycho!* she cried inwardly. *I've got to do something, and soon. Otherwise—*

"If jou scream, it's okay," he said matter-of-factly. "No one is here. The people who own this building are my comrades. They let me use it for my work. And that man I was with? He is gone too. My business with him is finished. Now, I have business with jou," he muttered, leaning forward with a cruel smirk. "Jou will tell me who jou work for, and I will be gentle. Or"—he slowly swiped the flat side of the blade against her throat—"jou will not tell me, and I will be very harsh."

Sydney swallowed as the knife continued to slide along her gullet. An intense fear was brewing in the darkness of her mind, but she pushed it back as far as it could go. Freaking out would only make things worse. Instead of meeting Sandoval's sinister gaze, she stared up at the ceiling tiles, the bone white fluorescent light tubes, and the dust-caked air-conditioning vent. Meanwhile, she wriggled her hands as fast as she could.

"What is wrong? Jou not going to answer, eh?" Sandoval laughed darkly, and she could feel his warm breath on her face and neck. "Okay," he said, sitting back and shrugging with the knife in his hand. "I guess we do it harsh."

Just then, her bindings gave way. Sydney tensed her body. This was it. She had to do something—*now*.

With one swift movement, she kicked out her left foot against his right arm. He crumpled slightly, dropping the knife. "If that's how you want it," she hissed. Then she grabbed the loose guitar strings and whipped them across his face as hard as she could. Sandoval cried out and fell backward.

Leaping from her chair, Sydney ran for the door, snatching the dagger as she went. She raced down the meandering corridors, her hair flying out behind her, trying to remember the path Roland and the others had led her down. Behind her, she could hear Sandoval's shouts echoing as he chased her.

Finally, the heavy steel door loomed in front of her. Sydney sprinted forward and threw her weight against it. But it didn't budge. Just like before, it was locked tight.

Sandoval's footsteps were now approaching down the passage. Whirling around, Sydney ducked through a nearby doorway and ran as fast as she could along the dim, cluttered corridor. There seemed to be no way out. In desperation, Sydney pushed down stacks of crates and knocked over spools of wiring, hoping to slow Sandoval's pursuit.

She was deep in the bowels of the arena. Sandoval had been right about the place being empty. Her only hope was to elude him long enough to find an unlocked exit, or until help arrived.

But who would come for me? she wondered as tears stung her eyes.

SD-6 were the only ones who knew where she was, and from the looks of things, she was on her own. And if she stayed out all night, Francie would only assume the party had gone terrifically well. She wouldn't worry for another several hours.

Come on, Syd, she ordered herself. *Get it together.*

The passage intersected with another, and Sydney took it. This one was slightly brighter, but much more cluttered. And as she ran, the ceiling seemed to slope lower and lower. *I must be under the stage,* she thought, stooping slightly. The place was a veritable obstacle course—a grid of steel supports littered with breaker boxes, the metal shells of unused spotlights, and long, snakelike cabling. Sydney carefully made her way through the debris, ducking under beams and sidestepping spaghetti-like piles of wire. She moved as soundlessly as possible, hoping Sandoval hadn't made the turn and was now dozens of yards down the other corridor.

A rattling noise sounded behind her. *"Mierda!"* Sandoval had followed. But at least his height seemed to be hampering him. Sydney mentally patted herself on the back for having taken off her boots.

"I know jou are here," he sang out sadistically. "I will find jou, *chica.*"

A burning anger raged inside her. Sydney resisted the urge to shout back, cursing him in the worst words she knew in five languages. But a voice in her head, which sounded amazingly like Yoav's, told her to stay quiet—to board up her emotions and focus.

The ceiling was now no more than four feet above the floor. Crouching further, Sydney sidled around a large wooden crate and came upon what looked like a small metal-gated elevator. The trapdoors! If she could ride one up to the stage, she could easily find her way out of the building. But where was the control panel? Her eyes followed a thick black power cord. It coiled into a shadowy three-foot-square crawl space directly in front of her.

Sydney dropped to her knees and crept forward. The space was dark and filthy and she kept scraping her elbows against the sharp joists of the stage's metal skeleton. Finally, the cable led her to a small black control box.

Excellent. Now all she had to do was pull it closer to the lift, activate it, and hop on before it pushed its way up through the stage. Clenching Sandoval's dagger between her teeth, she began to drag the power box by its cable back toward the platform. She was almost a foot away when a tall figure suddenly clambered into view.

"I told jou there was no escape," Sandoval hissed.

Sydney dropped the control box and snatched the dagger from her mouth, holding it straight out in front of her.

Sandoval let out a chuckle. Then he reached into his other boot and pulled out a small gun. "Jou think jou can stop me now?" he asked. He leaned casually against a steel girder, waving the weapon lazily in her direction. "I'd like to see that."

Sydney froze, staring into the shiny chrome muzzle of the gun. A 9-millimeter Ruger, she surmised. During the past several months she'd learned all about weapons. Their makes and models. How to load, shoot, and clean them. Even how to conceal them on her body. But Pilar had left out one crucial thing: how it felt when one was pointed directly at you.

She was vaguely aware of Sandoval muttering something, but she couldn't stop staring at the gun. She had somehow moved beyond fear into a detached, self-absorbed stupor. Was this how her life would end? A lot of good those months of training had done her. She knew she should be able to find a way out of this. But then fear slid down her throat, forming a cold, hard ball in the pit of her stomach, preventing her from moving. Speaking. Breathing. And only one thought kept echoing in her panicked brain.

I'm nineteen. And I'm going to die. . . .

"Now," Sandoval said, cocking the gun and correcting his aim, "jou will tell me who sent jou . . . or die."

A fog lifted off her. Sydney broke her gaze from the weapon and stared right into Sandoval's face. Her hand holding the knife was still raised. In a flash she brought it down and severed the power cable on the nearby breaker box. A searing pain ripped through her hands, but she somehow managed to grab the sparking end and hurl it against the steel beam Sandoval was leaning against.

There was an explosion of sparks and smoke, and a sound like ripping sheets filled the air. Sydney curled into a ball, shielding her head with her aching hands. And then all was silent. She looked up in time to see Sandoval slump forward onto the cement floor. Jets of steam rose from his back, giving off a sickening burning stench.

Sydney collapsed backward, her body wracked with deep, shuddering gasps. Everything that had happened at the arena slammed into her with the force of a Mack truck.

She had just killed somebody.

There had been no other choice.

For a long time she sat there, staring at Sandoval's sprawled form with a mixture of awe and horror and relief. The shorn end of the power cable jetted forth an occasional ember, like the last kernels of popping corn.

Then Sydney wiped her eyes and struggled to her feet. She made her way to another trapdoor platform and activated the switch. There came a whir of hydraulics, and then she was rising through the stage into the dark, noiseless arena.

She was free.

12

TEN MINUTES LATER, SYDNEY was running full speed down the sidewalk that skirted the concert hall. She had to call someone. But who? She was way too emotional to call Francie. And she didn't want to call Wilson, either. Obviously she must not be too important to SD-6 if they were willing to throw her into Sandoval's sweaty clutches without even preparing her.

Maybe she should call the cops. But if she did that, she could blow her cover with the agency and risk everyone involved. And that was if they even believed her. The truth was, they might very well see her as a murderer.

Because I killed someone, she screamed inwardly, a sharp twisting sensation wrenching her gut. *I actually* killed *someone!*

Or did she? What if Sandoval was only critically injured? She hadn't checked his pulse. For all she knew he was still alive. Whether he was a maniac or not, she should at least see that he got help . . . right?

She rounded the corner and flew down the wide concrete steps to the parking lot. In the distance she could see a row of pay phones under the bug-infested light of the streetlamp. Maybe by the time she reached them, she'd know who to call.

Suddenly, as Sydney stepped off the curb, a large van screeched to life from the cover of a dark alley.

There was no time to think who or why or what. Sydney put on a burst of speed and headed for a thicket of nearby trees. The van squealed to a stop behind her. She heard the sound of running feet. A few seconds later she was tackled to the grass. She kicked backward and jabbed with her elbows, but her arms and legs were held fast. She struggled. It got her nowhere. Two men in black ski

masks carried her to the van and threw her unceremoniously into the back.

One of the men shut the double doors and then
jumped into the passenger seat. "We got her. Go!"
he barked out to an unseen driver. The other at-
tacker crouched over her, holding down her wrists
and kneeling on her thighs.

With an angry grunt, Sydney tried to head butt
her assailant.

"Whoa. Calm down," the man said. "It's us."
Keeping an elbow on her forearm, he reached up
and ripped off his ski mask.

And Sydney found herself face to face with the
nameless SD-6 hunk.

*   *   *

"My god. What happened to you?" he asked, his
gaze traveling from her bruised face to her scorched
fingers on down to her dirt-streaked bare feet.

For a moment Sydney couldn't answer. Then
a sudden burst of anger exploded from inside her.

"What do you mean, 'What happened'?" she
yelled, struggling to a sitting position in the rocky
van. "I was tied up and threatened with a gun! I
was at the mercy of a lunatic! A lunatic you guys
sent me to see!"

The guy stared at her for a moment, his eyebrows knitting up in a look of . . . what? Concern? Annoyance? For some reason, Sydney couldn't quite pin it down.

He reached over and pulled the bracelet from her arm. "Aha," he said, turning it over in his hand. "That explains it."

"What?" Sydney snapped. "Your precious pictures are all there, if that's what you're looking for." There was no disguising the self-pity in her voice. She couldn't help it. It hurt to think that the agency was more worried about getting photos of a shady rock star than about keeping her safe. She'd thought they valued her. More than that, she'd thought they cared.

The guy let out a long, loud sigh. For a moment he just kneeled there, watching her, nodding slowly as if trying to make up his mind about something.

"Okay, listen," he said finally. "We're heading to SD-6 now for a debriefing, but I might as well tell you what was going on tonight. I think you deserve to know."

"I think so too," she said, lifting her chin defiantly.

The guy sat down beside her and ran a hand through his scruffy brown locks. "The truth is," he began, "the concert wasn't just a perk, as you were led to believe."

"Duh," she snapped irritably. She realized she sounded like a pouty kid, but she didn't care. Her hands hurt, her head ached, and the rest of her body felt as if it had been shoved through a mulcher. All she wanted was an explanation. A good one.

A wry grin breezed across his face and then vanished. "This whole thing," he mumbled, leaning toward her, "was just a test."

"A test?"

He nodded. "To see how capable you would be at handling a mission. And I've gotta say," he added, shaking his head, "I think you passed with flying colors."

Sydney pressed her fingers against her forehead. "But I don't understand. Are you saying this wasn't real?"

"Oh, it was real, all right. We've suspected for some time that Sandoval was selling information, using his status to gain entry into all sorts of countries. Unfortunately, he was also heavily guarded at all times and none of us had been able to get near him. But we did know he had one weakness—women."

"So . . . you used me as bait?" Sydney asked, scowling.

"Not exactly," the guy replied, propping his foot on the wheel well. "All SD-6 wanted was for you to go in and get close. Gather information. But they didn't want to tell you since you're not on full agent status yet. They were afraid if you knew, your behavior might inadvertently tip him off. First missions can be a killer."

"No kidding! Thanks to you guys, that's how I almost ended up!" She closed her eyes and sighed shakily. "Is Sandoval dead?"

He grimaced. "We'll find out soon enough. If he is, it's no loss to the world. Believe me."

"Why didn't they at least send some other people in to protect me?" Sydney whispered.

His eyebrows raised. "They did. There were agents in the arena who saw you go backstage, and we were outside in the van on electronic surveillance. We were tracking you through most of it, ready to extract you afterward, but we lost the signal during the concert."

"The signal?" she repeated quizzically.

He held up the bracelet and pointed to the empty socket where the green stone used to be. "The tracking device we'd planted somehow popped off into the pocket of another concertgoer, and we ended up following a couple from the Valley for forty minutes before we realized our mistake."

Sydney's mouth fell open. Her eyes blinked rapidly as a rush of thoughts and emotions crowded her mind. So they *had* been looking out for her. She really *did* matter. . . .

"I'm Noah, by the way," the guy said, thrusting out his hand. "Noah Hicks."

"Sydney Bristow," she replied distractedly. She reached out to grasp his palm and immediately cried out in pain.

"Sorry," he exclaimed, releasing his grip. He took her right hand in both of his and opened it gingerly. "Ouch. That looks bad. What happened?"

"It's a long story," she replied wearily. She watched his face as he bent over her injury. For the first time, she was able to really see him up close. A renegade lock of hair was hanging down the middle of his creased forehead. His high, chiseled cheek-bones quivered slightly as he pursed his lips. And there was a slight crook in his nose, making her wonder how many times it had been broken and how. Suddenly, her hands didn't hurt quite as badly anymore.

"Don't worry. We'll get you some help," he said, meeting her gaze. He leaned forward and called out to the driver, "How far away are we from HQ?"

"We're pulling into the garage right now," the driver replied.

"It'll be okay," Noah said, turning back toward her. "SD-6 has doctors on call at all times." Then he raised his hand and gently pushed her hair off her face.

Sydney sucked in her breath. A tingling sensation ran through her.

"Looks like you also got a nasty blow to the head," he said, frowning at her temple. "You'll want them to take a look at that."

Sydney deflated slightly, feeling incredibly silly. *Stop fantasizing,* she scolded herself. *The guy is just doing his job. It's not like it meant anything.*

Or *did* it? After all, didn't the manual say something about the significance of face and hand touching?

13

"OKAY. TELL ME AGAIN. So Sigmund Freud's cigar caught Marilyn Monroe's fur stole on fire, and you just decided to grab it *with your bare hands* and throw it into the swimming pool?" Francie's round eyes blinked in astonishment. "And you say you weren't drunk?"

Sydney shrugged sheepishly. "I know, I know. It was stupid."

Her story *was* pretty stupid. But it was the best she could come up with when she stumbled back into their dorm room, in bandages, twenty hours after she had left for the concert, and found Francie in near hysterics.

"Man, that must have been some party," Francie declared, shaking her head. "What a night. Terwilliger lets me out early. You get seriously burned. Jeez, is the world coming to an end or what?"

Sydney continued to sip her Dr Pepper, afraid to answer the question.

"So what about that guy you were checking out?" Francie asked, reverting to her typically bubbly self. "How did that go?"

"Oh, um . . . that was a bust. He turned out to be a real slimeball."

Francie flashed her a sympathetic look. "Too bad."

They continued their leisurely afternoon stroll through Westwood Village, sipping their sodas and taking in the crisp spring-afternoon air. Despite the occasional throbbing beneath her gauze wrappings, Sydney felt good. Incredibly good, in fact. Her debriefing at SD-6 had helped her push past the trauma at the arena, and the more she thought about it, the prouder she felt that she'd managed to get out of there on her own.

SD-6 didn't tell her much, which didn't surprise

her. Sydney didn't care. It was over, she was alive, and she had helped her country. The agency seemed very happy with the work she had done, especially linking Sandoval with Levski. Wilson had been really impressed too. And even though he didn't exactly say so, she could tell he was relieved she was okay. He had apologized for not being able to tell her the truth, and she had accepted his apology. He was only doing his job. She realized that now. "I really do have a daughter named Claire," he had told her, showing her a photograph of a smiling redheaded girl from his wallet.

Sydney had looked up at him. "I never doubted that you did."

Now Sydney and Francie paused in front of a bakery window. As she scanned the colorful display of assorted treats, Sydney caught sight of her reflection. Her long brown hair, although free from its customary clips, looked the same as always. Her tank top and capris fit the way they usually did. Even so, there was something different about her appearance. She seemed taller somehow, her movements more direct. And she was surprised to see a small smile on her face—something she hadn't even realized she was doing.

Could it be that she was . . . happy?

"Oh, I can't stand it," Francie cried, shaking her head. "I'm going to run inside and get one of those macadamia nut cookies. You want anything?"

"No, I'm fine," Sydney replied. "I'll wait out here."

As Francie disappeared through the shop door, Sydney strolled around the corner of the building. The combination brick-and-stucco wall at the side of the bakery served as an unofficial bulletin board for UCLA students, and it was constantly covered with promotional posters, job ads, lost-and-found notices, and *Roommates Wanted* signs. Sydney sucked the last of her Dr Pepper through the straw as she studied the flashy concert flyers. A band called the Numbers was playing at that trendy club near the Pier that evening. And she'd heard a lot of good buzz about the Bordersnakes, who were performing at the Lion's Den. Maybe she and Francie should go catch a show that night. It felt as if they hadn't been out together in ages. They could even invite Todd and get crazy.

All of a sudden, Sydney became aware she was being watched. Out of the corner of her eye, she saw a tall blond guy walk up and stop right beside her. He was pretending to study the wall of posters, but it didn't take a secret agent to know that he was checking her out.

It was Dean Carothers. His big green eyes and dimpled chin were as dreamy as always, and he looked even more tanned and muscular than before.

He turned toward her and smiled. Sydney braced herself for a rush of anxiety or anger or heart palpitations, but instead she felt . . . nothing. Not the slightest flinch. It was as if that horrible, humiliating encounter with him back in September had happened to someone else entirely.

"I hear the Bordersnakes have a new CD," he commented, nodding toward the funky promotional flyer.

"Yeah," she replied. She couldn't help wondering why he was talking to her. Did he need help prepping for finals or something?

"Are you a fan of theirs?" he asked, taking a step closer.

"I haven't actually seen them live yet," she said. "But what I've heard on the radio I like."

He flashed her another broad, toothy grin and leaned casually against the wall. "You really should check out a show," he said. "They're awesome."

"Right."

She toyed with her straw, waiting for him to pull a notebook out of his backpack and ask her about the summer class schedule. Instead, he held out his hand. "I'm Dean, by the way. Dean Carothers."

Sydney's eyebrows flew up. Was he actually introducing himself? *My god,* she thought. *He doesn't remember me at all.*

"I . . . uh . . ." She gestured awkwardly to her bandages. "I can't shake your hand."

"Oh, sorry," he exclaimed, his smile disappearing. He withdrew his hand and shoved it into his pocket. "What happened to you?"

She shook her head. "It's a long story."

"Well . . . why don't you tell me all about it at the club Saturday?" he asked, giving a modest shrug of his shoulder. He lowered his chin slightly, as if wanting to provide her the best possible view of his eyes. "You said you've never seen the Snakes live before. How about I take you?"

For a moment, Sydney stood silent. "Sorry. I'm going with other people," she replied finally.

"Oh," he said, his handsome face falling.

"Yep," she went on. "I don't know who yet, but someone else."

Then, with an innocent grin, she nonchalantly strode past Dean's shell-shocked form, rounded the corner, and headed down the sidewalk toward the bakery. A man sat on a nearby bench reading the *Los Angeles Register*. As she passed, a large block-type headline screamed out at her. ***Rock Musician Missing: Police Suspect Foul Play.***

Sydney tossed her empty soda can into a trash bin and stood gazing out at the bustling traffic. Francie had been right. Everything *was* different. Only the world wasn't coming to an end.

It was just beginning.

I've come a long way from the scared, vulnerable young woman I was last fall. I'm strong. Powerful. And I have a **purpose**.

And now I'm ready for more. I want to be challenged. I want to **save the world**. And I've finally found a way to do it . . . as an **agent** for SD-6.

One semester at a time.